# STRING LUG
# THE FOX

A BIG BROWN HARE LEAPED OVER HIS HEAD

DAVID STEPHEN

# String Lug The Fox

*Illustrated by*
NINA SCOTT LANGLEY

*Boston*
Little, Brown and Company

LIBRARY OF CONGRESS CATALOG CARD NO. 52-5005

FIRST AMERICAN EDITION

*Published 1952*

*Reprinted 1968*

PRINTED IN THE UNITED STATES OF AMERICA

FOR

KITTY AND JULIO

# Contents

# *Illustrations*

# Chapter One

## CUBS ARE BORN

O N A DEWY, GOLD AND GREEN APRIL MORNING, WHILE the owls were yet on the wing, the Summerfield vixen picked her way slowly along the pine-topped ridge which backboned the wood known as Mossrigg Strip from end to end.

She walked with her head low, her ears flattened against the sides of her skull, and her brush down between her legs, following the curve to her hocks. Her usual mincing gait was gone; her shoulders sagged; she was heavy with young and very near her time. Her one desire now was to get underground as quickly as possible in her burrow at the other end of the Strip. It was enlarged and ready: the deep, inner cavity was trodden hard and flat, and padded with many layers of dry bracken.

What caused her to leave the earth in the middle of the night is hard to say, for the dog fox had dropped a water-vole within easy reach of her before sunset; and he would certainly see that she wanted for nothing afterwards. Whatever it was, her first journey on leaving her warm bed had been to the Mossy Burn—a shallow, noisy stream with small trout, few pools, and spring-fed with water of an unsullied purity.

But it couldn't have been thirst that drove her out, for she lapped only a few quick mouthfuls as she waded across the broken water. Nor was it hunger for food. Certainly she nosed for a long time among the grass at the burnside, chewing with noisy click of teeth; and again, later, at the bottom of the ridge, she scraped in the soft loam under the rhododendrons, biting at the fibre in the soil. . . .

And now she was homeward bound, travelling heavy-footed on the crest of the ridge in the fire dazzle of the sunrise, instead of skulking through the thick rhododendrons and snowberries on the slope.

A hundred yards from home she halted—not suspiciously, but circumspectly—with her left paw uplifted like a pointer dog on game. Her nostrils quivered and dilated as she tested the wind fanning her face. She sorted out all the scents on the air, from the tang of moist earth and sweating pines to the thick smell of rabbits moving out to the open fields, and decided the road to her burrow was clear.

Through the forest of bracken ahead of her she pushed her way, to emerge showered with dew and ears itching with damp bracken dust. But she felt much refreshed from the chill wetting on her nose. Twice she dislodged loose pebbles on the whin scree and paused to listen to their minute clatter downhill. In the next ten paces she kicked a frightened frog, which she ignored, and crushed the pale, trembling cups of a frail wood anemone in a shady hollow. And there was the den at last, on the face of a grassy knoll, with five entrance holes and a great mound of earth in front.

The vixen's brush disappeared into the main burrow as a goggle-eyed rabbit burst from the one on the right. . . .

Not long afterwards the hazed sun was sending long, probing fingers of light into the innermost recesses of the Strip. Birds twittered in the thickets and Keewick, the tawny owl, sought the obscurity of his roost in an old pine near the fox earth. Flies danced in the dusty sunbeams. Gulls and rooks flew overhead in noisy array; the gulls to feed and the rooks to look for nest lining. The clack of a jackdaw slapped the morning in the face. Cushats crooned, and a cock pheasant crowed his summons to the lie-abed hens. Greyface, the old dog fox, entered the wood with the first birdsong, and went straight to his rock shelf on the ridge, a vantage-point from which he could watch the earth and eat his chicken in peace.

Greyface plucked feathers from his prize—a Buff Rock hen he had carried two miles in the dawn twilight. He never killed hens at Mossrigg. He was too wise to bring retribution on his head from Mossrigg, Summerfield, and Hackamore, the three farms in his immediate neighbourhood. Not yet, at any rate. Later on, perhaps; but at the moment, with a whelping vixen on his hands, he could not afford such easy, and dangerous, slaughter.

He was a big-boned, big-framed fox, hard and lean, almost gaunt, and totally unlike the fat-ribbed, small foxes of England. He was a true Scottish hill fox, belonging to a clan which knows not the protection of the Hunt, and with no one to pay for his sins except himself. Foxhounds he knew little about, having wandered only twice into hunting country; but he knew lurchers, greyhounds, terriers, traps, poison and guns—all the things which go to sharpen the wits and toughen the muscles of his kind north of the Border.

Of similar blood was his mate, about to give birth to her third litter. She was redder in the coat than Greyface, more finely drawn, and with more flesh on her bones. And if she was more rash, she was no less brave. His equal in stamina, she had less patience, and probably less real brain power—apart from sheer cunning. Greyface would have died for her, in spite of the fact that she had bitten holes in both his ears.

It took Greyface twenty minutes to pluck his Buff Rock to his satisfaction. Then he spent a long time on the breast, scraping the keel clean with his front teeth. When there was not a particle of flesh left on it, he bit into the abdomen to get at the liver, heart and entrails. He left the head, neck, feet and feathers. His meal over, he licked and licked between his toes till not the slightest trace of hen smell remained on them. Then he started to comb his great brush—with his teeth!

The vixen, meanwhile, was curled on her bracken bed with her brush round her nose and over her eyes. Her flanks rippled as spasms of pain passed along them. But it was late afternoon before her first cub was born—a tiny, mewing, squirming object, which she pummelled with her tongue till it was clean and dry.

By nightfall she had five cubs wandering with splayed forelegs through the soft fur of her belly. Twice, before midnight, Greyface poked his face into the nursery with food. He didn't wait to be thanked, for she snarled and chopped her teeth at him, and would have assaulted him had he attempted to stay. So he made a hasty withdrawal and trotted off to hunt field-mice.

The vixen's nose told her that he had left a young rabbit and another water-vole. The rabbit was the fresher kill, so she used it first. She did not want to leave her cubs just yet, and the fresh blood of the rabbit would save her a journey to the burn for water till later. She fed without disturbing her cubs. Reaching over her left shoulder, and using her right paw as a prop, she gripped the rabbit by the fud and jerked it in front of her. She ate it head first, devouring fur, bones and all, then fell asleep till daybreak, when a whine of greeting from outside told her that Greyface was on his way to his rock shelf again.

At noon she came out to drink and see if Greyface had left any further prey. He had. Just inside the burrow was a partridge, the chestnut horseshoe on its breast splashed with scarlet where the fox's teeth had bitten into its heart. Satisfied that she had enough for the present, she walked to the burn, a different fox from the one that had travelled along the ridge the previous morning.

Now her eyes were bright, questioning; her nose savoured the wind at every step; her muscles were tense, like a spring. Her walk was tight, almost stiff-legged, and the hair on her ruff was raised like that of an angry cur.

At the burn she lapped water till her flanks bulged. Though she raised her head only once during her drinking to look about her, nose and ears were alert for danger. A whisper of sound at her back made her wheel like lightning, the water from her jaws dripping to form tiny, sparkling globules on the waxy petals of the kingcups at her feet. It was Greyface. He was sitting with his tongue hanging out of the side of his mouth, his ears cocked and his brush curled round his right haunch.

But if Greyface felt in sociable mood, not so his wife! Being a vixen, she seldom did; and being a vixen with a newly-born family, she wouldn't, and couldn't, be. Greyface read the signs correctly, so that when she rushed at him, flashing ivory, he was already side-stepping, losing only a few hairs from his cheek instead of having his mask laid open. Then he discreetly withdrew. He knew the phase would pass in a day or two.

The wise old dog fox raced through the wood, and presently flung himself down beside a moss-grown, dry-stone dyke, where he began hunting for fleas in his fur. The vixen finished her interrupted drinking and loped back to her cubs. By the time Greyface ate his second flea she was again curled up with her family, who jostled each other as they mouthed for her nipples in the warm darkness.

She nosed her five cubs one after the other as they nursed, washing their faces and under their tails, in spite of their squeaks of protest. As a mother she was beyond reproach. Both her previous litters had gone into the world fit and well. She was as well known in the district as Greyface himself, principally for her flair for killing hens in daylight and slaughtering needlessly. She rushed in where Greyface chose not to tread. In a district where the names of farmers were invariably linked in speech with the names of their farms, she was known as the Summerfield vixen, which proved her notoriety.

In one afternoon she had slain eleven Buff Rock hens at Laverock Knowe. She once killed a ten-guinea Rhode Island Red cockerel beyond her usual range, and was credited with the slaughter because of her obvious signature. Then she crowned everything one frosty night at the beginning of the calling season when she chopped sixteen breeding ducks at Mossrigg. So she was much sought after; but, apart from some small shot in her brisket, she had so far escaped punishment. Already, had she but known it, her victims were looking for her— Gallacher of Mossrigg, Davidson of Laverock Knowe, Cameron of Summerfield, and the brothers McLeod of Hackamore, with their seven fox-hating collies and one Sealyham terrier.

And then there was Corrie—the shaggy blue Cairn; Corrie the Terrible, who had killed more fox cubs than he had teeth in his jaws; Corrie, the one four-legged creature she really feared; Corrie and his owner, Jock Simpson, the fencer, who had no special grudge against foxes, who knew more about them than all the others put together, and who was immeasurably more dangerous on that account when roused to action.

The vixen did not leave the earth again that day. Greyface, after luxuriating for an hour beside the dyke where he had sought refuge from his mate's bad temper, dawdled away to look at some rabbit snares he had seen set below the wire fence of the Mossrigg wheatfield. He trotted down the bracken-choked ride—over a quarter of a mile long—which divided Mossrigg and the greater wood of Blackcraigs, crossed two more rides at the Douglas and Brockhurst woods, and came out at the wheatfield beside the first of the snares.

Three cock pheasants whirred from the young wheat when he broke cover, crowing raucously as they rocketed

16

over the pines. In their wake rose ten cushats with a clatter of white-barred wings. Nearby, a magpie scolded from the fence-top. It bobbed up and down with flirting tail, and battered the stob viciously with its beak. Greyface grinned a foxy grin, because he knew why the pie was angry. There was a rabbit kicking in the snare.

Greyface knew exactly how to deal with such a windfall. He wasted no time on the wire or the peg of the snare, but set to work on the rabbit's neck right away. He had the head almost severed when he saw a man on the skyline, two hundred yards away, at the top of the rising ground of the wheatfield. It was Gallacher and his collie Nell, to both of whom Greyface paid the honour of his respect. They did not appear to be coming his way, but he withdrew into the shelter of the Brockhurst pines to watch them.

Gallacher, however, was not thinking about foxes— at least, he was not thinking particularly of Greyface. He was headed for the high pasture to look at his lambing ewes, hoping that all the lambs born in the night were on their feet with their mothers and that no fox was vomiting wool in the woods. Greyface returned to his rabbit when Gallacher disappeared. He had a clear conscience so far as lambs were concerned. He had no need of mutton. No fox needed to go hungry on his range; and at a pinch there were always hens. An odd hen was never missed by the farmers, a fact with which he was familiar, but one which so many of his kind failed to learn.

The foxy grin appeared again on his face when the snare noose hung kinked and bloodstained from the fence. Emptying snares was Greyface's hobby. And Pate Tamson, the rabbit-catcher, unkempt, unshaven, beer-soaked and tireless, was his special victim. The moocher hated Greyface, and cursed him and his forebears in the froth of many a pint of beer. Not that it made any difference. . . .

The rabbit's body Greyface kept for his mate; the head he ate himself. With little difficulty, he crushed the skull, devouring brains, teeth, eyes and fur, down to the last wisp of fluff sticking to his paw. For a moment he sniffed in circles round the snare, as though hoping to find another morsel of fur or brain, then he picked up the carcase in his jaws and left.

When he reached the ride at Mossrigg he slowed down to a walk, well hidden by the bracken and well content with his work. In one of the rhododendrons on the Black-craigs side a pair of cushats were building a nest four feet from the ground, a fact of which Greyface made a mental note, without, of course, giving the birds any idea that he had seen them. He did the same with Brushtail, the red squirrel, who was playing on a pine branch overhead with dry rattle of claws. Brushtail crouched, mute, when the fox passed underneath, and Greyface walked on without lifting his head, pretending he did not see. One of these days he would catch the chattering redcoat and save himself a lot of embarrassment.

Brushtail watched Greyface vault the dyke and pick his way along the top. He peeped round the pine trunk and saw him climb the ridge on a slant. Then he chattered bravely and volubly when the fox disappeared over the crest. Greyface did not stop to look back. He hated Brushtail and all his clan, and had spent many fruitless hours trying to catch, and silence, this particular nuisance. Even on sunny days in midwinter he was mocked from the leafless trees.

Keewick, the tawny owl, heard the fox come over the ridge and opened his great eyes to slits. When he saw Greyface he opened them wide, like saucers, and called *kee-wick, kee-wick, kee-wick* in a querulous, piercing voice. Thirty yards away, in another pine, his mate heard him as she drowsed on her five eggs in the old nest of a magpie. She peered over the edge with staring, liquid eyes, like a grave-faced cat. When she saw Greyface trotting towards the earth she immediately returned her attention to her eggs, for she knew him and had no reason to fear him.

Near the den ambled a great, fat rabbit, hunch-backed and carefree. Suddenly its nostrils twitched. It sat bolt upright, forepaws on chest and ears erect. Greyface came right on. The rabbit scuttered into the bracken, with white fud flashing, and Greyface stopped at the earth and dropped his stolen prize.

For a few moments he looked about him, then he barked, which was a most unusual thing for him to do at such a time of day. The vixen came out, shaking sand from her fur. She scratched her left ear with her left hindfoot, combed for fleas in her shoulder with her front teeth, then condescended to notice her mate, sitting with tongue a-loll and ears cocked beside his headless rabbit. And this time, instead of slashing him, she touched his nose with her own before taking possession of the rabbit and going back to her cubs.

# Chapter Two

*E*AST WIND IN THE NIGHT, A COLD CRANREUCH AT daybreak, and a sunrise without sun. In the east a thick wall of mist, suffused with dull crimson, smothering the tree tops. Over the fields a vast stratum of vapour, white and moveless; and the rimed grass and hedges draped with dewy webs of gossamer. Rabbit and hare tracks writ plain as in thin snow. A harsh edge to the sticky air. In the cushats' nests dead chicks—chilled while the old birds foraged early in the ploughland, not having the wit to wait till the sun lifted the frost from the trees.

Keewick, the tawny owl, sat on his pine roost with head bowed and breast feathers ruffled over talons. His craw was full of mice and he wanted to sleep. All night long he had hunted, while the high-sailing moon watched the hoar settle over woods and pasture, delivering five voles to his mate, now brooding a nestful of downy chicks.

But he couldn't get to sleep for the clacking of a jackdaw in an elm near the foxes' den. The bird had been going at it for nearly a quarter of an hour, watched from the top of the ridge by Brushtail, who stopped flaking a cone to listen. Every time the jackdaw called a blackbird pinked nervously, till at last Keewick turned his head to stare, full-faced and round-eyed, in their direction.

Right away he saw the cause of their excitement. Bunched together in front of the earth were five podgy little fox cubs, blue-brown and woolly, and bright-eyed as dormice. They couldn't see the jackdaw, but they were scared by his voice. Keewick, forgetting for the moment that he wanted to digest his mice, winnowed over to the

jackdaw's tree, soundless as a cloud shadow. As he settled
with dry scrape of talons, the jackdaw left, and a magpie,
which had been watching quietly higher up in the tree,
started to yatter. He stabbed his perch savagely with his
polished beak and plucked off leaves in anger when
Keewick folded his wings below him.

The fox cubs huddled together, sniffing and blinking
their eyes. They were afraid to move farther from their
doorstep. It was their first day out and their eyes were not
yet accustomed to the light. The new world somewhat
overawed them. Keewick looked at them solemnly, like a
cat. He decided they were of no interest to him, so he
returned to his tree; but not before he spied a hen blackbird on her nest below in the brushwood sheaf of the elm.
The pie knew about it too, and would rob it as soon as the
eggs were near hatching. At the moment he was engrossed in the fox cubs.

When Keewick wafted from his perch, the magpie
hopped lower, chocking and twisting his head to look at
the cubs with one eye. He was sorely tempted to fly down
and pinch their tails with his ebony beak, but with his
other eye he spotted Greyface on the ridge, sitting in the
shadow of Brushtail's tree. So he, too, left, chattering as he
flew.

Down by the burn, where the alders grew thick and
twisted and trailed their caterpillar catkins over the
water, the Summerfield vixen stopped to drink as she
came in from the grey fields. She was carrying a rabbit
she had caught in the whins near Hackamore at dawn, as
it tried to thump out the danger signal with its hind feet.
It had misjudged the speed of her rush, a mistake a rabbit
is allowed to make only once in a lifetime.

The vixen dropped her rabbit in a patch of yellow
celandines and lapped water. She lifted her head once,
angrily, when a dipper almost hit her on its swift flight
downstream. The bird cheeped and swerved, breasting

the chill water, and disappeared in the trailing mist.

With the rabbit gripped across the middle, the vixen waded the burn. The water was hock deep and chill. Minnows darted away from her paws as they slurred the loose pebbles on the amber bottom. Climbing out among the massed kingcups on the opposite bank, she almost trod on a water-vole which had its tunnel under the yellow screen. Keewick, in his tree, saw her as she bounded lightly over the wet grass under the alders and leaped the six ditches in the half-acre fir planting on the level ground below him. And he saw her drop her rabbit in the bracken near the earth before she went to her cubs.

The cubs mobbed her joyously when she appeared, prancing about with much stern-wagging; then they tried to get below her in a body. They became a confused jumble of legs and tails; they fell over each other and rolled on their backs, with paws in the air; they nipped, scratched and hog-shouthered with dug-in toes. The vixen danced and side-stepped. She reared and pirouetted, trying to find ground for her feet. She was carried several yards before she could jump clear and snarl an order that made them drop their tails and pin back their ears.

A moment's pause, while vixen and cubs watched each other; then she came and stood for them, with her hind-legs braced widely apart. They pushed under her almost as roughly as before, almost knocking her off her legs. With much noisy sucking and slughing, they started to nurse, sitting on their tails, stretching their necks to reach her, and treading with their tiny forepaws to make the milk flow. The vixen stood with up-pointed snout and curled lip, as baby claws punctured wrinkled skin, already scratched and sore from much previous pawing.

Two and a half minutes exactly she stood for them before she shook herself. Two cubs lost their grips and rolled over; the remaining three had to be dragged about six feet before they, too, lost their mouth-holds and fell sprawling. When the first two rushed at her to start all over again she defeated them by the simple expedient of lying down, lifting her lips when any of them tried to nose under her flank.

When she rose to fetch the rabbit she had brought for them, they made as if to follow her, but she ordered them to stay where they were and went alone. They became tremendously excited when they saw what she had. The vixen tossed the rabbit among them. They sniffed it and pawed it, and danced back and sideways, shaking their heads. They made furious pounces at it, pretending they were great hunters, and their mother grinned with pleasure. She could be very loving when they left her alone.

She started to break up the rabbit for them, tearing open the ribs and wrenching the hind legs away at the hips. The cubs' mood changed when they tongued the shining flesh. Nature had made them eaters of flesh, but it needed the taste of blood to betray the wild beast behind the puppy frolics. They snarled at each other and had their first bout of ear-biting. And still the vixen worked to dismember the rabbit, holding it with her fore-paws while she pulled it apart with her teeth. When it was reduced to a torn trunk, with head and legs severed, and green entrails spread on the ground, she vanished into the bracken and left them to it.

Five little fox cubs, uncovering baby teeth in baby snarls, backed away to five separate corners—three feet apart!—each with a piece of rabbit to gurry and grimace over, to protect from imaginary enemies, and, if possible, to eat. It was their first meal of real flesh. Hitherto milk had been their sole food, except for morsels of flesh licked up as questing noses found them. Now they were being truly blooded. In a day or two they would know all there was to know about eating a rabbit leg, and presently they would be able to tear up prey for themselves. From now on they would be nursed by the vixen twice a day, getting ever-diminishing quantities of milk till the source dried up and they were completely weaned.

Fox cubs are bold and inquiring. As cubs they have the will and the capacity to learn; as adults they possess the gift of memory and the ability to make up their minds. Lessons taught in cubhood serve them as guides to action in later life. The fox can put two and two together, is a supreme individualist, and is not the victim of blind habit or instinct. Rather is he a creature who weighs chances, ever ready to forsake outmoded ways to meet new conditions. So the cubs of Greyface and the Summerfield vixen learned as they grew.

Three days after their first meal of flesh they were well set up on their legs and making journeys of fifty yards from the den. They played and slept by turn, and frightened Brushtail so much that he fled into Blackcraigs for a rest cure. At first they came out to play only in the early mornings and late in the afternoon; but soon, realizing they were never molested, they were playing about at all hours of the day, only going below ground to sleep.

Their play was rough, and sharp baby teeth were often used in real earnest. From being mere rudders and nose-warmers, their brushes were soon being used for wiping an opponent's eyes—a trick dear to the hearts of all grown-up foxes. They fought in pair and trio; they fought four to one; and they fought in a general mix-up which tired them mightily and kept Keewick off his sleep. For playthings they used the remains of prey—foot of hare, wing of pheasant, head of hen. One cub, the biggest dog, had a rusty tin as his special plaything. It had been tossed nearby by a bird-watcher two years before.

Very jealous they were of their playthings. If a magpie sneaked in and tried to steal a bone to which a morsel of flesh still clung, they mobbed it in a body. Small birds hopping down to snatch wisps of rabbit fluff for nest-lining were likewise chased. The cubs no longer feared anything in feathers.

To roll about cuddling a favourite toy was sport they loved. Or to scamper hot-foot after leg of bird or hare sent spinning down the slope. Such practice developed their speed and judgment, the art of pounce and the accurate sweep of paw. But best of all they loved a tug-of-war—five to a pheasant wing. And this helped to loosen their baby teeth, which would soon be pushed out by the pressure of budding ivory fangs.

As the days lengthened and the black buds of the ash trees at last burst into bloom, the cubs became bolder in their journeyings, till they were climbing to the top of the ridge or trekking almost right down to the fir planting by the burn. And as muscles toughened and confidence grew their journeys became more frequent. The desire to find out things, to explore, was growing in them. They wore a maze of runways in the bracken beside the earth, frightened the rabbits away from nearby burrows and caused a little wren to desert her eggs. Even Keewick changed his roosting tree to another pine some distance along the slope.

Both Keewick and his mate were now hunting. Their chicks no longer needed brooding, being twelve days old and able to keep themselves warm. The cubs became familiar with the owls, with their hooting and yelping when they swept into the wood with prey, and with their ghost-like shapes flitting through the trees in moonlight or gloaming. And they came to listen for the wheezing of the owlets in the nest not far away, although they had not the remotest idea what they were like.

One thing the wideawake cubs did learn—that quite often dead mice were to be found at the bottom of the owls' tree, tossed overboard when the owlets scrambled

25

for the prey. And so, in the intervals of waiting for their parents, the cubs paid attention to the owls, running to the tree every time Keewick or his mate touched down at the nest. In this polite form of theft they learned early that shrews were not good to eat, and declined to touch them.

On a night of full moon they found an owlet on the ground below the nest. It turned over on its back and clutched at them with its talons when they nosed forward. They made no attempt to paw it or bite it; but three times in the night they went back to find it still there, huddled disconsolately on the same spot, cold and hungry. The next day it was still there, but at night it was dead, with blowfly maggots already crowding its eyelids. Neither Keewick nor his mate had ever attempted to feed it. The cubs wrinkled their snouts and refused to touch it.

At half-past eight the following morning, when the wood was gleaming with reflected sun sparkle, the biggest cub trotted right down to the burn, leaving the rest of the family basking in a sun circle beside the mouth of the den.

Not only was he the biggest and strongest cub in the litter; he was already a little tousie in the coat where russet fur was ousting baby wool. He went to the burn because he had often seen his mother come from that direction. Perhaps he hoped to find her there. He crossed the wet levels, bright with starry celandine and lilac of cuckoo flower, and found himself in the half-acre fir planting.

It was there he met the Mossrigg tom-cat—Satan. . . .

Satan was a great, hulking, moon-faced killer, with a heart of stone and a soul steeped in sin. He was the greatest poacher in the parish. He had enormous curved claws, like the talons of an Arctic owl, pointed sharper than the canine teeth of a weasel, and a forearm stroke like a wild cat. He had once killed a hare bigger than himself. Gallacher of Mossrigg swore that Satan had no

THE CUB ROLLED OVER IN A FROLIC

heart, and that he hadn't been born, but quarried. . . .

Satan hated every living thing except Gallacher's collie Nell, and the mistress of Mossrigg, for whom he contrived to purr.

The cub sidled up to Satan, with his stern curved right round till it was almost bumping his own face. But Satan sat like an image. The cub frisked closer. Satan stared expressionlessly. The cub rolled over in a frolic, legs in the air.

Then Satan struck.

Poor cub! No wild-cat could have surpassed the indescribable savagery of Satan's assault. The cat was fur-clad murder, with four fists full of living fish-hooks unsheathed. His lips lifted, baring his gums. He clawed and ripped with his deadly forepaws, heedless of the shrill *ee-aye: ee-ow: ee-aye-aye-aye-ee* of absolute terror from his victim.

The cub was pinned to the ground. He squirmed and grovelled, and furrowed the damp earth with his forepaws as he kicked and screighed in a very ecstasy of terror. Cushats rose with leathery slap of wings at the disturbance. And still Satan's claws drew blood.

Fortunately for the cub, he cowered on his side, with his paw movement protecting his exposed eye. He got his flank ripped in several places, his jaw slashed, and his right ear cut almost to ribbons. His mouth was cut, and his gums earth-soiled and bleeding. And he had three punctures in his belly. Satan would assuredly have killed him, for Greyface and the vixen were far away. It was Jock Simpson, the fencer from Mossrigg, who saved his life. He had been working at fences across, and down, the burn, and came running when he heard the yells of the cub.

Satan whisked away among the fir saplings at sight of the tall, broad-shouldered man with the brown dungarees and the weather-beaten face. The cub, instantly realizing that his tormentor had gone, tried to bolt, but Jock gripped him by the ruff before he could get into his stride. He spanned the bleeding muzzle with his strong fingers, in case baby teeth tried to bite. Then he examined carefully every wound on the cub's body.

"Poor wee eejit," he exclaimed as he fingered the cub's bloody right ear. "Where's your pa and ma? Didn't ye ken that Satan fights wi' twa handfu's o' razors? This is a nice right lug ye have noo, chewed up like string. Ye'll no' be cockin' that yin again, I'm thinkin'."

Jock reflected as he held the struggling cub, which was now trying hard to bite him. Should he knock it on the head? There was no doubt about it: he should. Yet he hadn't the heart to kill it in cold blood. In its mauled state it appealed to that side of him which made him spend long nights in midwinter watching foxes. As an individual he had no grudge against foxes; as a countryman with some knowledge of the economics of farming he often killed them. Hence his logical inconsistency.

Finally, he put the cub down.

"Now, wee String Lug," he said. "Show me where your hoose is. Ye can have your chance this oncet, but ye'd better look sharp when the dugs get busy."

Jock watched the cub disappear into the bracken, and was satisfied. He would have to let the farmers know about the earth, of course. Much as he would have liked a closer look, he had too much sense to approach any nearer. The vixen would probably move the cubs if she found his scent too near at hand. So he left hurriedly, in case she was watching him even now.

He hoped fervently that the smell of his hands would have left the cub by the time she came to lick its wounds. He had been wrong, after all, he thought, to turn it loose, perhaps ruining any chance there was of catching and destroying the family. Yet he was curiously free from any sign of remorse.

# Chapter Three

## STRING LUG SURVIVES

STRING LUG'S ONLY SERIOUS INJURY WAS THE ONE TO his right ear. It hung over, ribboned halfway down from the tip, and was a red glaze of blood. By the time the vixen came it was hard and black-clotted and shrivelled. He had no stomach for food and watched the others nurse for their two minutes without the urge to join them. And, of course, his mother knew at once that he was requiring her attention.

Very tenderly she licked his flanks, his belly and his face. Her lips drooled saliva when she came to his ear, and she tongued it just long enough to prevent a fresh flow of blood starting. Every time another cub came near her she warned it off. Her work on String Lug finished, she bundled them all roughly underground. She wanted to reconnoitre.

By morning twilight String Lug felt much better, though his ear was hard and heavy. His spirit was too electric to stay dumped for long. His wounds he had almost forgotten; the cause of them he would never forget.

It was he who found the plump young wood-pigeon, lightly covered over with earth, which Greyface had left down earlier, and which he had stolen from the nest he had seen being built in Blackcraigs on the day String Lug was born. String Lug fought with the other cubs for sole possession of the prize. He got it. But they didn't stop trying to steal it from him till the vixen arrived with a young hare, which she hid in the bracken so that they would have to quest for it.

String Lug tore off feathers from his prey, just as he

29

had seen his mother do. He chewed slowly, however, for his jaws were yet stiff, and hurt when he over-stretched them. But he succeeded in eating the best of the pigeon.

He played with the other cubs afterwards, yelping when they clawed his torn ear. The vixen came back, empty-mouthed, and sported with them for perhaps twenty minutes. String Lug fell out of the game before she left, and nosed scents. His ear was ticking. There were no enticing smells, so he lay down on the mound in front of the den and watched the vixen rough-housing with the rest of the family. When she trotted away, the cubs lay down to pant and rest. String Lug went to earth to nurse his ear.

Late in the afternoon he lay on the slope above the den, on his belly, with chin resting on forepaws. He was in no mood for the company of the other cubs. He lay with his eyes closed to slits, but his good ear was wide open. A rustle in the bracken made him open his eyes wide and cock his left ear. A low-set, snaky animal, with brown fur and a wicked, triangular face, rippled in front of him like a gigantic caterpillar. It was Whittret, the weasel from the dyke on the other side of the ridge. What he wanted on ground so heavily tainted with fox smell, he alone knew.

String Lug rose and chased Whittret. He had no fear of the small beast, but he disliked the look of him. Whittret chattered like tapped pebbles and hissed as he bolted. String Lug was ready to hit out with his paw when Greyface burst from the bracken, nosing Whittret's scent line. Whittret saw the big fox just in time and found a convenient hole, as weasels always manage to do. Grey-face's chopping teeth almost caught his tail as he disappeared. The fox pawed the hole, sniffed, snarled, and left when String Lug raced to greet him.

String Lug had seen the dog fox so seldom that he wanted to fuss, and be fussed over. In his excitement he barked, his first effort and the first by any of the family. Of course, it was not a real, honest-to-goodness bark: in fact no fox would have considered it a bark at all. But then he was still a baby, wearing baby fur, and a month ahead of schedule. It was such a good effort, however, that it brought Greyface back to nose over this amazing son of his. String Lug was delighted. He pawed and jumped at the great grey beast, who might at last have stayed to frolic had not a yell from up the slope rent the air at that moment. Greyface vanished, and String Lug dived into the burrow. For it was the sort of yell he himself had uttered when he fell foul of Satan. . . .

Presently the howler came home, trailing a splayed hind leg. Climbing up to Greyface's shelf to get a closer look at Brushtail in a tree, the cub had lost his footing and crashed down on the scree. He dislocated his hip—a disability with which no fox cub could possibly hope to survive.

String Lug felt a sort of kinship for little Splayleg— whether because they were the only two dog cubs or the only two injured is hard to say. At playtime Splayleg did his best, but he was now such a slidder, and in such pain, that he had to fall out. String Lug stopped at the same time. They lay down together, nose to nose, and boxed gently with their forepaws. But even this was too much for Splayleg, so they had to give it up and be content with nose-biting.

The vixen could do nothing to help the new sufferer, nor did she seem able to appreciate fully the seriousness of his injury. During the night, unable to fight for his share of the food, Splayleg had to be content with the leavings. For String Lug's affection for his injured brother did not take him to the stage of sharing his food with him.

The next day String Lug and Splayleg stayed together, while the young vixens nosed trails in the bracken or played with their mother. Once they tried to reach the blackbird's nest in the elm tree, which now contained young chicks. But they only succeeded in frightening the hen so much that she stayed away for nearly two hours, returning just in time to save her family from death by chilling. She brought off her brood without mishap in spite of the fact that Greyface knew of the nest and could have emptied it at any time, had he wished to do so.

Four days after his accident Splayleg was stiff and pining. String Lug, his own wounds now almost painless, tried hard to make him play, without success. There was no devil left in his brother. Death was certain for little Splayleg; but, as it happened, he was not to die lingering in pain.

A party of five men crossed the burn near the fir planting early on the following Sunday. The morning was bright and chill, with the trees gleaming wetly and glinting gold. Jock Simpson was first across the burn, followed by Gallacher of Mossrigg, Pate Tamson, Cameron of Summerfield, and Andrew—one of the lads from Laverock Knowe. They had no misgivings about doing their work on a Sunday, Gallacher asserting that "the better the day the better the deed". And it was inbred habit that made them come at peep of day, rather than later, dragging Jock from his bed in spite of his protests that a couple of hours would make no difference, as the vixen would not be at home, anyway.

Jock had the three-year-old Corrie at his heel, along with the Laverock Knowe Sealyham terrier, Flossie, an inexperienced yearling with more bounce than fight. The two Mossrigg collies, Nell and Glen, slouched behind Gallacher, who, like Cameron, was carrying a shotgun of the hammer type, already loaded and cocked.

"So you haven't been right up at the den?" asked Andrew, who had only heard of the expedition when the terrier was called for that morning.

"Naw," replied Jock as he stooped under the firs with

the terriers dancing at his heels. "I watched the cub. The auld bitch would ha'e moved them if I'd went any closer. But we'll no miss the place, never fear! There'll be plenty o' somebody's hens lying aboot advertisin' it!"

Gallacher swore. He often swore. It suited him. He was a great, good-natured horse of a man, of the hearty type who wear open-necked shirts in midwinter and have hands insulated against the cold with callouses and horsehair. He was clean-shaven, fifty and a non-smoker.

"Whit for Jock wanted tae let that cub awa fair bates me." He winked at Cameron, who was the heron type, hammered out on an anvil. "He gets a' sentimental aboot they foxes at times. But I say, chap them on the heid!"

"Jis-so; jis-so," said Cameron. "It's the best. . . ."

"See this wee flooer?" Jock butted in. "Shuts its leaves in the cauld, sensible cratur! It'll open them when the sun gets through. And there's the Summerfield vixen yonder, slinkin' up the scree. Smart move that o' hers, puppin' in Mossrigg and us speirin' for her in Summerfield. The cubs'll be in the hole by this time. An', Wull!" He turned his humorous grey eyes on Gallacher. "I'd let that wee cub awa again. Ye canna grudge me an odd cub. I must ha'e something tae keep me oot o' bed at night."

"Funny notions," murmured Cameron.

But Gallacher guffawed. He always guffawed when the fencer poked fun at him. Then he exclaimed, quite seriously: "Man, I widna bother the beasts mysel' if they'd leave the hens alane. But this killin' fair gets my goat!"

The vixen kept to the ridge top, a hundred yards away, watching the men and dogs. She had no fear of the dogs where she was; but she feared for the safety of her cubs. And there was nothing she could do about it. Gallacher kept the collies to heel. They had no chance of running her down in the woods.

The party stopped to watch the vixen. Gallacher spoke: "See how she keeps oot o' gunshot, Pate!" The moocher jumped at the sudden shout. "That wee .22 rifle o' yours! Could ye cop her at that far?"

Pate hesitated. "Mebbe. This is a smooth bore. I micht try."

"You'll only cripple her wi' that," Jock interrupted. "Let her be. She'll mebbe dodge near enough when we send the dugs doon." But as he spoke Pate had fired. The vixen jumped and disappeared from the ridge.

"Send the dugs, Wull!" Pate shouted. "I nicked her!"

"Let the dugs be," said Jock, speaking to Gallacher. "She'll only hole up if they chase her. And Corrie's no boltin' ony wounded vixens. Save the collies' braith."

As they pushed their way through the bracken, now beginning to collapse and green-shot with new growth, Jock and Gallacher picked up the remains of kills—hares, rabbits, hens, partridges, rats. Several ragged wings lay in front of the mound at the den mouth. Cameron of Summerfield shook his head.

"This foxes canny be bose," he said. "They're better off than some bodies, and nothing to pay for their misdeemours." Cameron was a philosopher who related all things to money, and a master at abbreviating polysyllables to suit himself. . . .

"Well! What's the programme?" asked Gallacher. "What age d'ye reckon the cubs is? I mean, are they wee enough for Corrie tae manage?"

Jock rubbed his chin. He reckoned the cubs would be about seven weeks old, and he was sure Corrie would manage to deal with them. At his suggestion, Flossie was tied up. Gallacher and Cameron were to stand above the den, with guns ready. Pate thought the collies should be left loose in case a cub broke out and tried to escape, but Gallacher would have none of it.

"Naw," he said. "I don't want them loose among guns.

They can bide wi' me. They can easy be sent efter a runaway."

"Corrie!"

As Jock spoke the terrier's name, Pate suddenly lifted his rifle to his shoulder. He was taking aim when Gallacher spoke. "What are ye shootin' at?"

"There's a hoolet in that pine there. I'll blast its . . ."

"Blast *you* for an eejit!" roared Gallacher in his best hayfield voice, pulling down the rifle. "Whit fur d'ye want tae shoot an owl? Man, can ye no see a bird withoot wantin' tae blaw its heid aff? You're worse'n a gamekeeper!"

Pate spluttered in confusion. "But it kills young rabbits an' . . ."

Gallacher interrupted him again. "Well, good luck tae it! That's supposed to be your job. An' I seen a body writin' in the papers aboot hoo many rats and mice owls killed in a season. Jist leave them be. If they foxes wid stick tae killin rats an' rabbits—aye, an' even phaisants—an' leave my lambs an' pooltry alane, I widna be botherin' *them* either! Phaisants is as bad as the cushies in the spring an' back end."

"Man, Wull," said Jock, laughing, "that's terrible talk for a fermer. Phaisants is protected by a' the laws o' God an' man; an' foxes maun dee if they touch them, whether they kill your hens or no."

"That'll be right," muttered Gallacher as he went to Keewick's tree to have a closer look at him. "This is the first time I've been this close to an owl. Queer joukers, whit? An' they foxhound packs is only a farce," he shouted suddenly. "Supposed to be keepin' doon foxes! An' yet that keeper freen o' Summerfield's here sends loads o' them tae England every year tae keep up the supply."

"Jis-so," Cameron started, "but . . ."

"But nothing!" Gallacher was in rare fettle. "They micht as well be honest an' admit they protect the beasts

35

because they like gettin' dressed up like Boer War sojers an' chasin' them wi' a wheen o' dugs. If a fox bothers ye, shoot it! If it disna, then ye've nae need tae be botherin' it."

Jock Simpson laughed. "Everything you say's true, Wull. In fact, you're only a parrot quotin' me. But d'ye want this hole cleaned oot the day? Or wid ye raither wait an' separate the phaisant killers fae the hen killers at a later date?"

"Let's get started," said Gallacher huffily. "Send Corrie doon!"

Cameron and Gallacher took up their positions above the earth, with the collies at heel. Andrew and Pate stood beside Flossie, who was tied to a rowan sapling about four feet high. Jock told Corrie to seek them out and at once the shaggy Cairn nosed the holes. He stopped at the main entrance, grinned at Jock through the long hair on his face, wagged his pointed tail, and disappeared.

In the deep nursery chamber of the earth five cubs huddled against the solid whin wall at their backs. They could hear the voices of the men outside, strange sounds which they did not recognize and could not understand. But they were afraid, nevertheless. And, presently, another and greater fear gripped them when they caught the first puff of Corrie's scent as he scrambled down the twisting burrow. Almost at once the dog's nose located the terrified cubs as they cowered in the warm darkness.

Corrie started to bark. It was a girning snarl of a bark, with a skirling edge to it, which filled the burrow with harsh music. The cubs squeezed tighter together— terrified, helpless and silent. . . . Outside, the men knew by the crescendo of barking that the terrier was rushing to the worry. They heard his sudden gurry-wurry, throaty and muffled; then silence. And they knew the Cairn had killed.

In a moment the dog came out, tail first, wriggling

his haunches as he struggled back. He was dragging a twitching fox cub. It was Splayleg, pushed to the front by the others as they tried to struggle away. The Sealyham danced on her hind legs, straining at the string and barking furiously. Andrew shouted at her, but had to slap her down to quieten her.

Jock took the dead cub from Corrie and sent him down again. Once more they heard his skirling bark, then his well-known gurry; and he soon came out dragging a second cub. Flossie became frantic, and tried to bite Andrew when he cuffed her down. The collies sat grave-eyed and silent behind Gallacher and Cameron, both of whom looked very far from happy. Pate picked up the two bodies and carried them aside, out of the way. Jock turned to Gallacher.

"Keep your eyes skinned for the grey dug, Wull. He'll no be far awa, and mebbe the bitch as well if she's no sair hurted."

"Jis-so; jis-so," murmured Cameron, turning to look uphill.

Corrie came out with a third cub. He had blood on his muzzle, not all of it belonging to his victim, for he had been nipped by one of the remaining two cubs as he worried. When he was dragging out the fourth cub Jock suddenly dived sideways at the holes on the right, and struggled on the ground as if he had taken a fit. Cameron exclaimed: "Goodness, gracious!" when Jock rose to his feet holding a struggling cub. It was String Lug.

"See that," he shouted, "tryin' tae scramble oot the back door when he knew it was his turn. This is the cub I turned loose!"

"The wan wi' the torn lug," Gallacher exclaimed. "The wan Satan near massacraed. Man, man!"

"Seems to be the last of them," observed Cameron in his staid way, as Corrie jumped about with his tail describing circles, showing no further interest in the holes.

37

Jock suddenly got his eye on the body of Splayleg. "There's anither hurted cub," he said. "Hm! A twisted hip. We did it a good turn!"

Pate stuffed the four dead cubs into a bag which Andrew held open for him, then he tapped Jock on the shoulder with his grimy hand.

"Will ye gi'e me that cub, Jock? I ken yin that'll pay me thirty shillins for it. I'll split it wi' ye."

"Best kill it," said Gallacher practically.

"What aboot it?" Pate persisted, thinking of the thirty shillings. "Fifteen bob apiece. It's flingin' money away if ye kill it."

Jock handed him the cub. "Ye can have it, Pate, an' the thirty bob as well. I'm pleased tae see the cratur spared at that. I've took a kind o' shine tae the beast, but I daren't keep it mysel, what wi' the wife's hens."

Pate tied String Lug's forelegs and hindlegs together and held him under his arm. The party made ready to leave. There was no sign of the vixen, or Greyface: but neither of them was very far away. Greyface was hidden in the fir planting by the burn, ill at ease, restless, but realizing the hopelessness of trying to interfere. Over in Blackcraigs the vixen lay beneath a tattered windfall, lick-licking at a broken forepaw.

"Well," said Gallacher, "we'd best get started back. Drap they cubs in the midden, Pate; unless ye ha'e a use for them. And keep that torn-lugged imp a hunner mile fae Mossrigg. Nell! Glen!" he shouted to the collies. "Come in ahint!" And he started down the slope. Jock called Corrie, turned the Sealyham loose, and with the others followed Gallacher to the burn.

Greyface was back at the earth before the sound of the men's voices had died away. He came quietly, at a crouching run, looking furtively over his shoulder at every step. At the earth he paused, his nose wrinkling at the taint of men and dogs on the air. And his nose told him much of the story; though he went underground to confirm its judgment. When he came out he wasted no time looking about; nor did he go to Blackcraigs to look for the vixen. He trotted away on the trail of the men and dogs who had wrecked his home.

And there was silence at the den except for the rustling of leaves stirred by a freshening breeze.

# Chapter Four

## RESCUE

------

*P*ATE TAMSON LIVED WITH HIS WIFE, FIVE CHILDREN, back smoke and a blue lurcher in a two-roomed rickle of a house, surrounded by a straggling elder hedge, about a mile and a half from the Mossrigg earth. The east gable was packed with uncemented bricks. At the doorstep was a grated drain, milk-glutty from the passage of much soapy water. A narrow lane led to the house, flanked by high hedges and two strips of tail pines.

There were two sheds behind the house, and two orange-box hutches with ferrets. One of the sheds was packed with tools, poaching and rabbiting gear; the other was overcrowded with several varieties of hens, mostly stolen from distant farms during poaching forays. For Pate was a man of parts, being miner, farm-worker and poacher by turn. He shot pheasants at roost, netted partridges, dynamited salmon and caught roe deer in snares of fencing wire. The local farmers accepted him because he really could kill rabbits and did a horse out of a job at harvest-time.

Pate put String Lug in a rearing coop which had housed a Rhode Island Red hen and eleven mongrel chicks, all of them flea-ridden. The coop was floorless, Pate having read somewhere that chicks did best in contact with the earth. This, apparently, was all the instruction he was capable of absorbing, for he kept the coop on the same spot all the time, so that the ground was baked and sour. String Lug had no special objection to the smell of his prison; but he was afraid, and refused to show himself in the wire-netted run attached to the coop when there was anyone near him.

Left to himself, he spent all his time trying to find a way out, rearing on his hind legs and pawing round and round the cavey with his forefeet. He kept it up for a couple of hours, and finally flung himself down in the comparative darkness of the coop and slept from sheer exhaustion.

At tea-time he was offered a bowlful of white bread, soaked in milk, which he refused. This surprised Pate, who, like so many of his kind, had a fixed idea that the young of flesh-eating mammals can thrive on a worthless mixture of white bread and watered-down milk. When Pate went back to the house, remarking, "He'll eat it afore it eats him," String Lug resumed his two-legged tour of his prison.

At night he was shut up in the coop, the drop door being tightly wedged against the front with two rusty iron bars. They, in turn, were wedged to the ground with two heavy stones, while on top of the coop Pate placed a fifty-pound weight. He was determined that the cub would not claw its way out or overturn the coop. When he went to bed he was satisfied with his work and sure of collecting his thirty shillings on the morrow. All of which goes to show that Pate had a plentiful lack of knowledge concerning foxes.

The moon was high when Greyface and the vixen skulked down the lane to the house, hugging the hedge shadow. The vixen was travelling on three legs, carrying her left forepaw, which was swollen and painful. To the west the sky was ruddy from the glare of a tapped furnace in the steelworks. Bark of dog, hoot of owl, shrill whistle of locomotive came from afar; but the foxes did not pause to listen.

Greyface approached Pate's house from the front, with the vixen at his heels. They leaped over a smelly ditch, choked with rank grass glaucous as rhododendron leaves, and paused in the shadow of the elder hedge. The front window of the house was silvered in the moonshine. A hedge sparrow chirped and whirred away with rustle of leaves. In the hedge bottom a shrew squeaked as it chewed a wriggling earthworm. Greyface pawed his lower jaw as rough leaves of mustard scraped his muzzle, and nosed down the hedge. The vixen took the opposite direction. They met at the back, having circled the house, and their noses at once located the imprisoned cub.

Pushing through the hedge, Greyface blundered into a clump of stinging nettles which forced his head up and his brush down. In his tracks came the vixen, her usual impetuosity cooled by the ache in her foot. Scent of beans in flower, heavy odour of hens, moonlight and heavy shadow, and no sign of life. In a basin of water the moon's image shimmered and shuddered. Shadows of foxes moved along the wall outside Pate's window, four feet from his head as he slept, and in another moment String Lug's parents were at the coop, with ruffs up, heads down, and noses and ears alert for danger.

Unable to paw at the coop with her injured foot, and unable to stand on it while she used her good one, the vixen had, perforce, to sit on her tail and watch the dog fox work to release the cub. Greyface didn't waste any time on the woodwork. He started to dig under it. The thud-thud of his paws was loud enough to start the hens chuckling throatily, in question, but not in fear, and not quite loud enough to waken the lurcher sleeping under Pate's bed.

In a few minutes Greyface had made a hole big enough to allow him to touch noses with String Lug on the inside. The cub soon added to the noise by clawing at the woodwork above his head. The earth showered between Greyface's hind legs as he burrowed deeper and deeper: he had loose soil on fur, eyebrows and tongue, which he tried to shake off each time he paused to look over his shoulder.

42

THE VIXEN SAT LICKING HER BROKEN PAW

The vixen sat, impassive, licking her broken paw. Grey-face dug a hole just big enough to allow String Lug to squeeze out with much twisting and wriggling. They spent no time in greeting, though String Lug was ready to fuss. Through the hedge the vixen squeezed, followed by her cub. Greyface paused for a moment to sniff at the closed pop-hole of Pate's hen house, and snarl noiselessly at the ferrets, before following his family.

The foxes must have had a prearranged plan for the next moves; just as surely as Greyface, returning from trailing String Lug's abductors, conveyed his where-abouts to the vixen, and took her to the pine strip to lie up till it was safe to rescue him. In the pine strip Greyface took the lead. Pushing under the bottom wire of the fence at the hayfield, he stood aside till his family joined him. Then he led them to the burn, which at this point made a wide loop before flowing eastwards to Mossrigg.

Greyface worked on the assumption that Pate's lurcher would soon be on his trail. The dog had a good nose. This the old fox knew, so he proceeded to confuse his trail, to tie his scent line up in knots.

Entering the water, now very shallow after so many dry days, he splashed downstream with his family for two hundred yards. When they climbed out on the opposite bank, he retraced his steps, travelling for perhaps a hundred yards upstream beyond his original line of entry. He came out of the water on the same side, raced for fifty yards or so, then retraced his line to the burn. This time he went right across, casting a loop till he was opposite the point at which he had originally led in the vixen and cub. Back into the water he went again, trotted downstream, and clambered out at the same spot where his family had already gone ashore.

He grinned his foxy grin when he caught up with his family. The lurcher would have bother sorting out that puzzle. If there was one thing Greyface could do better than emptying snares, it was knocking dogs dizzy following their noses in circles which led nowhere.

The foxes crossed the next field quickly. They skirted the farm, quiet and peaceful in the moonlight, crossed the road, and found themselves in the small pasture where the calves were put out to grass in summer. At the bottom of this small meadow they met the burn again, but this time they crossed without any trail-faking. At the top of the next field was Hackamore Wood, their destination. . . .

In the field thirty Ayrshires grazed or lay chewing the cud, and a hedgehog hunted the tussocks, directed by his snuffling snout. The foxes were mobbed by lapwings calling *pees-weep*, *pees-weep* as they swept down on humming wings. The cows started to follow at a shambling trot, with heads down and noses snorting. Rabbits bolted for the wood when they got a whiff of the tainted air, for Greyface was travelling downwind. Past the crowded molehills on the wood edge, into the ditch, through the fence—and then the moonlit gloom of Hackamore, where Greyface left the party.

String Lug was put to bed in an old burrow beneath the stone- and earth-packed roots of a fallen pine, about twenty yards from the pasture fence. It was a burrow Greyface often used in the winter. The vixen denned up in a scrape under a rowan tree in the heaviest cover of Hackamore, where the ground was much broken up and sloped steeply to a wet and bracken-choked glen. And, somehow, Greyface knew where to find both of them when he came along in the grey, rain-threatening dawn with food. To String Lug he brought a rat, which he had caught in the Mossrigg Farm stackyard as it scurried from woodpile to wheatstack.

Being very hungry indeed, String Lug soon made short work of the rat. He was very greedy and messy about it, chewing with the hurried anxiety of a dog with a too hot potato, soiling his black forepaws and getting his whiskers crimsoned with blood. He sniffed about when he had finished, pink tongue curling over stained teeth, and then went to bed without attempting to clean himself.

He slept for two hours, nose to flank and brush curled over eyes, and was awakened suddenly by the sound of a man's voice and the barking of dogs. The fear he had known when Corrie raided his old home returned to him. He became panicky and was almost tempted to bolt from his burrow and run for his life; but he overcame the impulse. The instinct to wait and see, to weigh chances before taking action, was strong in him. So he lay still, listening. . . .

The voice he heard was that of Colin McLeod of Hackamore Farm, shouting instructions to his two collies as they rounded up the cows for the milking. The dogs barked as stubborn beasts refused to move, nipping tender heels, and jumping back as outraged cows lashed out with cleft hooves. In a few minutes thirty cows were plodding in single file to the gate at the road, followed by Colin and his black-and-white dogs.

String Lug very soon realized they had gone. He came out of his hole very cautiously, sniffing the air and pricking his left ear to listen. A squirrel flashed up a red pine tree as he poked out his nose, and he heard the scratch of its clawed feet on the branches overhead. The loud crooning of cushats, the fluting of blackbirds, the twitter of swallows hawking flies above the trees—he heard them all. And he also heard a hissing as of escaping steam, which was the breathing of the wood.

Ten paces away, in an open space, was a splash of sunlight, from which white vapour rose as the warmth dried out the pine needle carpet. String Lug lay down on this warm patch to bask and clean himself. He scraped his face and snout with his paws, starting behind his ears and working forward to his nose, till all sign of his recent meal had been cleaned away. Afterwards he fell to licking his forepaws till they shone blue-black with the wetting from his long, warmly-moist tongue.

But he was still hungry—and lonely. He missed the company of Splayleg and his three sisters. And where was his mother? It was time she was here to frisk with him and teach him fox tricks. Yet he didn't pine, for he still had one thing—his curiosity. And that is a great deal to a fox cub.

He was curious to learn about the new world into which he had come after such terrifying experiences, to find out if Keewick or Brushtail were there, or the noisy jackdaw. Perhaps he would even find the rest of the family, for he was not very clear in his mind as to what had actually happened. He hadn't a single plaything to box, or maul with his paw. So he started to explore—slowly, cautiously, with two eyes, two nostrils, and one ear all alert for danger.

At first he kept to the piles of grass- and bracken-covered branches and brushwood which cluttered the ground, peering round trees and continually testing the air. Once he tried to cross an area of emerald green moss, but turned back in fear when he felt it quaking under him. He sunk hock deep as he back-tracked and came out with his legs dripping black ooze. After smelling once at the soiling, he left it to dry and flake off by itself, making no effort to lick it clean with his tongue.

Nosing a ragged heap of fir sheddings, he was nearly frightened out of his wits. With a crash of rotten branches, and dust spurned from powdery twigs, a big brown hare leaped right over his head and fled for the open fields. The hare raced with ears flattened and big hind pads gripping the earth ahead of forepaws. He misjudged the height of the wire at the fence and it quivered as he hit it with his high rump on the way underneath.

But if the hare was frightened, String Lug was terrified, and he fled back to his burrow without waiting to nose the hare's bed. In his excitement he lost his sense of direction and he had to cast about for some minutes before he found the fallen pine.

The vixen came to him when the cows returned to the pasture after milking. Her paw was still swollen and painful, and the wound leaking. String Lug, unfortunately, chose the sore paw to bite on, causing her to whip round on him and snarl so close to his face that he felt her hot breath on his muzzle. She tried to rough-house with him, to teach him to grapple and hold, but the wound in her foot was continually being knocked. So she gave up and left String Lug to himself again.

In his subsequent questing he found—of all things—an old boot, with rusty tackets, no toe caps, and grass growing through the lace holes. As he jerked it from its grassy anchorage a little blue and yellow bird alighted on the dry ground below a white willow and disappeared into a mousehole. String Lug at once dropped his boot and scampered to the hole. He tried to push his nose in, but the hole was too small. And it was too small to admit his paw. So he started to dig like a dog at a rabbit hole, biting at the fibre uncovered by his nails.

Naturally he was very much taken aback when the little blue and yellow bird flew out and hit him on the nose. But he was sufficiently alert to chop at her as she swerved away from him. Piqued at his failure to catch the blue-tit, he was turning back to retrieve his boot when Greyface appeared, suddenly, from nowhere. String Lug danced round him, but Greyface pushed roughly past to the mousehole. He sniffed loudly, as though he would extract the contents by inhalation. Then he started to dig.

String Lug capered round him as he dug, wondering what it was all about. Didn't his father know the bird had gone? What a waste of time and energy! Digging at an empty hole! For String Lug thought he could teach the wise. But it was he who was surprised when Greyface

47

uncovered a tiny nest containing no less than nine scrawny, gaping, baby blue-tits. . . .

For a few days afterwards String Lug nosed every mousehole, hoping to find little birds in them. But he soon came to realize that blue-tits nesting in mouseholes are very exceptional beings indeed. His examination of mouseholes taught him one thing, however. He learned that, besides mice, such burrows often sheltered weasels, and had his nose nipped by Whittret one day when, undeterred by the musky smell, he poked his nose into a burrow.

It was about this time he learned, too, that there were other foxes in the world besides his parents. One day he ventured to the south fence of Hackamore and into the hayfield which stretched the entire length of the wood. The thick cover of the hay, now nearly ready for cutting, appealed to him greatly, and he became excited at the scents of rabbits and voles around him. Settling down to follow a rabbit line, he came out of the tall hay again, nosed among the buttercups and clover and vigorous stems of hogweed, squeezed through the fence once more, and found himself face to face with a red fox—a vixen; an old vixen with yellowing tusks, no family, and a heart as spiteful as Satan's.

String Lug backed away. He knew at once that this beast was deadly. But he was not allowed to escape unscathed. As he turned to run she rushed at him, missing his good ear by a hair's breadth as her teeth click-clicked. She chased him through the wood, nipping at his heels, and twice furrowed his flank with her tusks. Near the patch of emerald moss she ran almost full tilt into the Summerfield vixen. String Lug's mother rushed at the assailant. With her disabled paw, however, she was in no state to inflict serious damage; in any case, the strange vixen did not wait to argue after the first nip in the cheek.

And so the days passed for String Lug, each with its

incident or its little excitement, with lessons learned the hard way, for he saw little of his mother. Greyface brought food to him several times each night, hiding it so that he had to quest for it and dig it up for himself. And this made him use his nose more than ever, and taught him the advantages of burying surplus food till it was needed.

The red and ochre leaves of the oaks turned pure green and tips of burnished gold brightened the sombre hue of the pines. Each dusk a corncrake called to its mate in the hayfield—the last of their kind in all that region. Swallows touched throats with their own colourful water images as they sipped water on the wing. Beside String Lug's tree a queen wasp worked in a mousehole, moulding pulp to the roof to form the top story of her nest. Heavy rain came with the first blue of the speedwell in the hedgerows, flattening the hay and filling the ditches with gurgling, discoloured water. In the clearings of Hackamore yellow pimpernel and bedstraw appeared, and the hayfield fence became a tangle of hedge-mustard and stitchwort, hogweed, Jack-by-the-hedge, and cleft-petalled red campion. In the thickest parts of the woods kids of roe deer cowered, wet and shivering, their mottled hides providing the only sun-spots in a gloomy world.

String Lug passed the rainy days in the wood. Once he wandered into the hay, but he got his fur so wet and full of hayseed that he did not go back again while it lasted. The trees dripped and swallows hunted low. The grass at the gate of the pasture was stamped into a squelchy mass of mud by the Hackamore cattle.

Then one morning the sky cleared, blue as the petals of the brooklime in the wet hollows, and String Lug took his boot into the pasture to play. The sun soon dried the grass, and brought out the flies, so that String Lug spent more time pawing them as they buzzed about his ears than he did playing with his boot. Except for two short spells when he went to his burrow to sleep, he spent the whole day among the molehills in the pasture. And he was there at dusk when the vixen came limping up the woodside, carrying a small rabbit in her jaws.

Thirty yards from String Lug the vixen stopped, and faced the wood. String Lug didn't yet see her, but she saw the man standing behind a tree just inside the wood, with a shotgun under his arm. She dropped the rabbit, walked forward six paces, looked from the man to her cub and— sat down! She watched the man lift the gun, point it at her, slowly, deliberately. The roar of the gun sent String Lug helter-skelter to cover without looking to see what had happened. And from the other side it brought Jock Simpson and Colin McLeod at a run.

The man behind the tree was Gallacher of Mossrigg. He emerged from his hiding-place and was climbing the pasture fence when he was joined by the others. McLeod also had a gun which he uncocked as Jock Simpson vaulted the fence and lifted the vixen by the brush.

Gallacher swore as he stood his gun against the fence and scratched his head.

"It disna make sense!" he remarked to the others. "For she saw me, sure as she's lyin' there deid."

"But what happened, Wull?" asked Jock and Colin at once. "How'd ye cop her? She didn't just walk up and ask ye to shoot her!"

"But that's just it!" said Gallacher vehemently. "She came right up when I was swithering whether tae shoot the cub. And then I'll be damned if she didna march right in front o' me, sit doon, and let me blaw her apairt! An' the cub bolted before I could turn the gun on it."

Jock nodded. "Likely that was her idea. An' the cub'll be the wan Tamson lost." He turned to McLeod. "Well, Colin; it's a good job ye saw the cub playin' in the field this mornin'. That's the last o' the Summerfield vixen, but she'd never ha'e done much good wi' that paw."

Gallacher was not convinced about the vixen's behaviour. "Look, Jock," he said. "She could've warned the cub withoot comin' in gunshot o' me."

"Sure, man, sure! And ye'd ha'e shot it the meenit she opened her gub. Nay, man. I'm sure she did it on purpose tae save the bit cub. It's the only way it makes sense!"

"Will the cub dee?" asked McLeod. "She must be feeding it yet. . . ."

"Hardly. It's mebbe young enough tae hunt its lane yet, but it's got a faither. An' dug foxes can be guid faithers: especially this dug. Best plan's tae get Corrie at daylicht and find the sett right away. Otherwise there'll likely be a flittin'."

But Greyface did not wait for dawn and Corrie. At moonrise he came for String Lug, after his nose had told him the story of his vixen's death just as surely as if he had been there to see, and led him from Hackamore to the wood where his mother had spent the greater part of her life—Summerfield.

# Chapter Five

## ALONE

SUMMERFIELD WAS A GREAT, RAMBLING WOOD OF mixed growth, with the Mossy Burn almost cutting it in half, and a drystone dyke running along that part of it which edged the road. At three points it was deeply bitten into by fields. The ground was rough, hillocky, and undermined in the dry places above the burn with rabbit burrows. Most of the trees, as in the other woods thereabouts, were pines. But there were sycamores, elms and birches aplenty—the birches mostly near the burn and in well-defined groups; while on the edge of the water grew alders and hazels, with here and there a gean resplendent in perfumed white blossom.

At one point, near a heavy plank which spanned the burn and was used as a footbridge, there was a clump of nine cedars, so thick that it was always twilight under their heavy screen. One of the cedars grew from the base of a stony mound. In its branches a waterhen nested every year, at varying heights from the ground, her downy, soot and vermilion chicks simply bouncing from feathery branch to feathery branch on their way down to earth. Stones and earth had been moved from the roots of the tree on one side—probably by the last badger in all those woods—leaving a hole just big enough for a fox to squeeze into. And it was here that Greyface brought String Lug, by a roundabout route from Hackamore.

String Lug didn't like the new burrow. It was too cramped for one thing. And the ground below the cedars was permanently soggy and puddly. Besides, the heavy perfume from the jungle of wild liquorice on the banks of the burn did not appeal to his nostrils, though the scent of aniseed released when he bruised the silver-splashed leaves was not displeasing to him. Then he saw a man passing down the opposite bank at eight o'clock in the morning. He was a labourer, going to work; but String Lug's experience of men up till then had not been re-assuring. So he quit, and moved farther down the burn.

He found a new shelter without difficulty, a simple couch under the gnarled roots of a sycamore which had been blown down by a gale years before. The place was dry and open to the sun. It was String Lug's first real move on his own, the first time he had made up his own mind. It signified his growing ability to look after himself, and gave him a feeling of confidence. And before the day was over he had made his first capture.

Nosing among the thick growth by the burn when the sun was turning the trunks of the pine trees blood red, he spied a furry, beady-eyed beast nibbling willow shoots at the water's edge. The water-vole did not know of his presence and gnawed greedily. She had a family of hungry youngsters in a burrow across the burn. There was a crescent scar, like a white thread, on her flank where it had been scored by the talons of Keewick in the spring. Keewick had just managed to escape a ducking when he tried to clutch her from the water with his foot.

String Lug flattened as soon as he saw the vole. He squatted on his belly, on his elbows, and with his left hind leg stretched out behind him, hock uppermost. The wind came from the vole to him, and his nostrils savoured its musty, warm scent. There was only one obstacle between him and his prey—the prostrate trunk of a birch sapling, long fallen, with its bark bright and clean, though the heart inside was rotted to cork and powder.

The vole chewed on as String Lug wormed stealthily nearer. He gathered his hind legs, getting a firm grip with his pads, and sprang. He hit the birch sapling, shattering its middle to brown and silver splinters, and tumbled down on the startled vole. Wheeling instantly, it tried to scurry to the water, but String Lug's forepaws pinned it before it could reach the pebbly shallows. The stroke was a lucky one, for he had been completely off balance when he delivered it. But he felt proud of his prowess. He had caught the vole unaided: there was no question about that. And it tasted twice as good in consequence.

Squatting on the bank, with his rump against a lichen-covered stump, he devoured his prey, holding it with his paws as he chewed. For some reason, he did not eat the head. Instead, he used it as a plaything, pawing it as a cat does with a mouse, until he knocked it into the water. He watched it sink to the bottom, rolling with the current among the barred and chequered shadows on the blue and amber bottom. When it was washed under the overhanging bank he promptly forgot all about it.

In the course of the next week he made three more kills —a water-vole and two mice. They were paltry enough trophies for the amount of craft and energy he expended on them, but his confidence increased with the number of his kills, so that he began to spend more time prowling than playing. At twilight on the eighth day of his sojourn in Summerfield he discovered the hayfield in a horseshoe bend on the south side of the wood. The first few cuts had been made by the reaper, and cutting proper would begin on the morrow.

String Lug trotted up the woodside cut, watching rabbit after rabbit bolting into the hay at his approach. And he discovered that the hay was swarming with mice, rustling and squeaking as they scampered about on their mousy affairs. The place reminded him so much of Hackamore that he forgot about his den by the burn and pushed his way into the hay. He liked the place—the sweet smell of clover and hay, the rabbit and mouse smells, the weak scent of the birds which had foraged there earlier. But above all, he became aware of a strange, new smell, a thrilling odour which he had never known before. It was the scent of a roe doe and her twin fawns, which she had removed as soon as the men left after cutting the first swathes of hay.

Greyface did not come in the night, not because he didn't know where to find his son, but because he knew the cub was now able to fend for himself. String Lug, naturally, knew nothing of the dog fox's desertion, and waited patiently, somehow hoping he would turn up: but he made no attempt to return to the wood. Instead, he stalked rabbits in the hay, till he was finally rewarded by catching a very small one which crouched with flattened ears and made no effort to run.

Next day, about the middle of the forenoon, he was perturbed to hear the sound of men's voices and the whir and rattle of machinery. The Summerfield men had come to cut the hay. There were two men carrying guns in the party, ready to shoot rabbits bolting from the thick cover.

String Lug spent the next two hours in an agony of fear and apprehension. Afraid to bolt, he sat listening to the rattle and clatter of the reaper as it moved round and round in ever-narrowing circles. The sun shone; men cursed the flies; the smell of hot oil and metal stank in String Lug's nostrils; and all the time the area of standing hay shrunk in size as the tractor circled, noisily, monotonously, relentlessly. . . .

String Lug was almost frantic. He could hear the tread of the men with the guns as they walked round with the tractor. And still his cover shrank. Guns roared, reloaded and roared again as rabbits broke cover and tried to bolt. And then a voice was shouting: "There's a fox in there, Geordie! Make another turn and stop. This one's in the bag. . . ."

That was a moment of panic terror for String Lug. He was in as tight a corner as he had been in when Corrie raided the Mossrigg earth: and he knew it. Fear spasms rippled along his flanks as he stood with drooping rump and hanging brush, listening, and showing the whites of his eyes. His pose was rigid, statuesque, but a little comical, for his left upper lip was tucked inside his left lower tusk, so that he appeared to be laughing. But he didn't feel in the least like laughing. Men he now recognized as supremely dangerous. Though he understood not a word of what had been said he knew from the excitement of the voices that his presence had been discovered.

Geordie stopped the tractor on the narrow end of the cut, leaving the engine ticking over. Blue vapour puffed upwards like a heat haze from the exhaust as it went *blub-blub-blub: splutter-splitter.* String Lug knew the tractor had stopped moving even before he heard the thud of Geordie's boots as he jumped down from the driving seat. Then he heard his hurried instructions to his companions. . . .

"We'd best drive fae end to end, boys," he was saying. "You, Mr. Sinclair, take the right-hand corner at the ither end. I'll walk wi' Alec fae this end, an' keep him on my left on the edge of the cut. If the fox rins the full length ye'll get him as he breks oot. If he comes oot on wan side, yin or ither o' ye'll get him, for ye'll ha'e baith sides covered, an' nathur o' ye'll be mair than twenty yairds fae him. When ye see him, gi'e him everything ye've got! Right?"

And so they placed themselves. Geordie and Alec started from the tractor end and walked slowly through the thick hay, Geordie with his thumbs in his braces and Alec with the barrel of his shotgun resting on his left forearm. Both men were keyed up, with eyes alert for the first sign of a fox, while Sinclair at the other end stood almost on tiptoe in his eagerness to see everything.

String Lug crouched flat till Geordie and Alec were almost upon him; then he started to belly-crawl ahead of them, scarcely disturbing the hay in his stealthy passage.

Neither man saw him because of the high hay and his low posture. But before he had travelled fifteen yards in this fashion String Lug realized that he was walking into Sinclair's arms. He stopped, and almost broke away in panic. Which way? Was there any way? Oh! he had so little time to think. . . .

He raised his head to look. There they were! He flicked his wet tongue over his ivory teeth, turned, reflected, made up his mind, and . . . well, it was all over in a bewildering handful of seconds.

Crouching low, String Lug streaked back in his tracks, with neck stretched⸱ and brush flying. He shot past Geordie's leather-clad legs as Sinclair shouted: "He's breaking back!" Alec flung up his gun, but couldn't shoot because Geordie was in the line of fire. Geordie, startled, kicked out at String Lug as he flashed past, missed him, and fell heavily in the hay with his legs in the air. String Lug was through! Geordie swore and Alec's gun roared when the angle was safe. But the shot was too far behind. It zipped off timothy heads and holed the wings of a dancing butterfly, but didn't harm String Lug. He tore on, flat out, realizing that speed was the prime essential now.

A second shot ripped hay at his heels. He broke cover beside the tractor just as Sinclair, who had sprinted up after shouting his warning, appeared at the corner of the cut. String Lug bolted under the spluttering tractor as Sinclair's gun belched death. The roar of it shocked the air. String Lug came out on the other side as pellets spattered and tinkled on the metal and poofed and peenked into the heavy rubber tyres. Away across the lying hay went the fox, faster than a sheepdog, and running with the airy grace and lightness so characteristic of his kind.

They tried a long shot at him as he ran, but the pellets dropped far behind him, holing some dock leaves standing above the flattened hay, and scattering loose, granular soil from a solitary molehill. String Lug crashed through the wire fence into Summerfield, without looking back. He was quivering with fear and excitement. His heart pounded so furiously that it made him dizzy, though he was fresh as a May morning and could have run for miles. For the first time in his life the musk smell was strong on him, bearing testimony to the fact that he was no longer a baby.

A few yards inside the wood he halted, and listened. It took him only a few seconds to realize that he was not being followed, so he turned back to the fence, very cautiously, and scanned the hayfield from the shelter of a great tree trunk. For String Lug had the curiosity complex, just as much as the rabbit, the weasel and the deer. Only, he was master of it, not its victim. Curiosity is life and knowledge to a fox: it is rarely the death of him. . . .

String Lug was beginning to enjoy himself watching them. The thought of spying on men at such close range unseen, tickled his sense of humour—or whatever it is that passes for a sense of humour among foxes. But his pleasure was shortlived when he saw Alec and Sinclair pick up their guns and start walking right in his direction. He presumed they were coming to hunt him again— always a safe presumption on the part of any fox—and bolted. Of course, the men had no idea that he was anywhere near. They had simply decided, in a half-hearted way and for want of something else to do, to scour Summerfield on the long chance of seeing him again.

Had he been as old as his father, String Lug would simply have stepped aside and lain low, since the men had no dogs with them. Instead, he bolted fast through Summerfield, much faster than he had any need to do, in his anxiety to get away from them. Through a grove of silver birches he passed, under a smother of alders where the wet ground sucked at his pads, till he reached the burn. Water! It was an age-old instinct of his kind that made him seek it, to foil the noses of any who might follow. For water is the great scent-eliminator.

Slithering through the clutter of vegetation on the bank, where the perfumed, fluffy cream blossoms of the meadow-sweet, swaying on wine-red stems, grew thickest, he leaped lightly into the shallow water. Perhaps he chose the meadow-sweet tangle as a point of entry in the hope that its pervading perfume would blot out his musk scent on land. He walked and trotted downstream, lapping water hastily, slipping on sun-burnished, oozy stones, and stirring up mud among the green, translucent weeds trailing and snaking in the current.

Trout and minnows darted into stone shadows as he disturbed them, and great dragonflies, gauzy-winged and bejewelled in rainbow mail, darted and hovered above his head. A tiny sedge-warbler, performing acrobatics in a clump of yellow iris as she hunted flies, almost flew into his jaws with fright as he turned out of the water among the glistening spears.

On the bank he shook water from his belly and brush fur, and pawed a fly from his eye. Then he set off up a mossy slope where snowberries grew thick under the high, shady canopy of pines. At the top of the slope, flanking the road, was the Summerfield drystone dyke, dilapidated and moss-grown, and screened with tendrils of bramble along most of its length. String Lug jumped on to the dyke, and stood for a moment with all four feet bunched closely together—a striking silhouette against the sombre pines on the other side of the road.

He didn't like the open glare of the road. He crossed to the other side, leaped on to the dyke, and slithered down the slippery, water-blackened stones on the inside. There was a green strip between dyke and wood, where dog-rose and vivid fireweed crowded close. String Lug pushed through into the gloom of the pines and was momentarily startled by the leathery clap of wood-pigeons' wings which greeted his arrival. The wood at this point was narrow, and he was soon through it, in the golden daylight, to find himself on the edge of a wide, hillocky stretch of ground, covered with whin, gleaming waxy yellow in the sunshine. His lingering anxiety about being followed vanished when he beheld the multitudes of rabbits among the whins. They were everywhere —ambling, nibbling, face-washing or sitting hunch-shouldered at burrow mouths.

String Lug flattened instantly, and eyed them longingly. Here was food; abundance of food; and he was hungry. Strange, but he hadn't noticed it till then. But the nearest rabbit was twenty yards away, and his own position was too open. A crow, flying overhead, spied him and cawed a warning; but the rabbits, after sitting upright for a moment, paid no further heed to it.

Very stealthily, String Lug wormed his way along the tree fringe—in a series of quick crawls with intervals of rigid stillness between them—and, presently, gained a screen of yellow flowers, the stem shadows of which broke up his outline. But his prospects of catching a rabbit seemed little brighter. He thought, and thought, and thought. Then he thought again. No! He could still make nothing of it. The nearest rabbit, a half-grown doe, was fifteen feet from a burrow and fifteen yards from the fox. String Lug knew a rush was out of the question. The rabbit would be halfway down the burrow before he could cover those fifteen yards.

The sun was hot, flies buzzed in his ear, and his patience was running low. Unconsciously, he began to twitch his tail—like a cat in the beginning of anger. Before long it was sweeping from side to side in slow, steady rhythm. . . .

Suddenly the nearest rabbit sat up and gazed in his

direction. String Lug pressed flat against the damp ground, scarcely daring to peer through the wiry stems in front of his face. But he still continued to wag his tail. The rabbit kept staring, goggle-eyed, wrinkling its cleft nose in a scenting query. And then—wonder of wonders! —it started to hop slowly towards him, hunch-backed and ears at ease. String Lug trembled involuntarily. But, wait! There were three others looking up . . . moving . . . beginning to follow the first one.

Were they going to come and give themselves up? It certainly looked very like it. . . .

String Lug could scarcely restrain himself. Twelve yards, eleven yards, ten. . . . The suspense was almost unbearable. String Lug, with an effort, kept control of every muscle in his body—except his tail. All at once he realized it was moving. Curious, though, when he stopped twitching it, the rabbits stopped moving forward, and sat up with ears pointing to the sky. Then it suddenly dawned on String Lug that it was his tail they were interested in. . . .

Very gingerly, he twitched the grey-white tip of his brush, and sure enough, after a minute or so, the rabbits came on again, with their great big silly eyes staring foolishly, and their ears at the *at ease* angle.

The first rabbit was within twenty feet of String Lug before its brain received a danger signal from the sixth sense which sometimes watches over the destiny of rabbits. It was galvanized into action as String Lug shot from his hiding place, with all the power of his hind legs behind the thrust. He was among the startled rabbits before they got properly into their stride. With a deft sweep of his left paw, he bowled over the first of them, twisted round, pounced and chopped—all in the twinkling of an eye. As the rabbit rolled over he snatched it up. It kicked, squealing shrilly and piercingly as his jaws closed on its ribs. Its squealing stopped; it twitched, died, rolled its eyes, grated its incisor teeth, treaded with its forepaws, and went limp in his jaws.

And when String Lug looked round there was not a single rabbit to be seen above ground among the whins.

String Lug left his bed at the same time as Keewick, the tawny owl, swept from his tree in Mossrigg to begin his night's hunting. The western sky was suffused with dull crimson and gold, and the swifts still sailed on wide wings in the high, cool air. Keewick hooted twice as String Lug followed a deer path through a bracken-choked hollow, and the first bats wavered among the trees. String Lug nosed a rabbit trail and settled down to follow it, more out of curiosity than hunger. On the edge of the ride between Brockhurst and Blackcraigs he stopped abruptly, with left ear cocked and nostrils dilated.

*Thud—thump—thud!*

The sound came from behind a whin boulder on the other side of the ride. String Lug flattened, and belly-crawled in a semicircle to get into the wind of the boulder. Strange! The smell was fox. He moved up towards the boulder inquiringly. The thudding stopped: so did String Lug. In the next instant a fox dashed into view. Greyface! He had been clawing at fleas in his neck fur, and the thudding sound was caused by his foot walloping the ground between every other scratching stroke. Greyface came out bristling and snarling. He rushed at String Lug as if to shoulder him, and chopped wickedly at his jowl before turning away, stiff-legged and truculent.

String Lug fled in shocked amazement. Was this girning, bad-tempered beast his father? There was no doubt about it. But it was a new Greyface. Right through Mossrigg Strip the outraged cub raced, and down the ridge past his birthplace till he reached the burn. He crossed dry-foot by using a flat boulder in the middle as a stepping stone.

That brief encounter with Greyface taught String Lug a lesson which he might otherwise have had to learn more painfully—that all foxes of the same sex are enemies throughout their lives. The lesson upset String Lug considerably and completely spoiled his night's hunting. The only thing he caught was a field-mouse, which he managed to pin down with his paw in a grass tussock. Sniffing later among the wild valerian by the burn, he flushed a waterhen, and made the mistake of following her when she fluttered in mock disablement across the water. By the time he turned back to her nest on the water's edge all that was left was the warm, tantalizing smell of birds, the downy chicks having tumbled into the water when their mother lured the fox away. He contented himself with rolling ecstatically among the valerian for several minutes before setting off for home.

For a week afterwards rain fell almost continuously, and String Lug left his soaked bed to den up under a rock overhang a little distance away. He scraped up the pebbly soil till he made a saucer-shaped hollow, into which he could snuggle comfortably. Not yet was he ready to seek an underground lair. String Lug became very fond of his new den: it was sheltered from the rain and wind, caught the sun for three hours in the morning, and was always perfectly dry.

Here it was that he saw his first roe deer, a doe and two mottled fawns, and learned that they were creatures of fairly fixed habits, passing that way every morning at the same time. The dainty, playful fawns intrigued him greatly, but he knew they were dangerous game for him and made no move to show himself. So the roe passed each morning, unaware of the fox which watched them from twenty yards away. String Lug was inclined to treat the roe as mere woodland adornments till one morning, passing through a little clearing in Blackcraigs on his way home, he had an experience which completely changed his outlook.

Prancing gracefully round a scrub birch in the middle of the clearing was a handsome roe deer doe, followed by a haughty, high-stepping, six-pointer buck, whose name was Bounce. A little distance away, standing under the low, feathery branches of a young spruce, staring with liquid, wondering eyes, were the doe's fawns. They were puzzled by the behaviour of their mother and the buck which pursued her. Doe and buck had satin-sleek red coats and white patches on their throats. They had already worn a distinct path round the tree when String Lug arrived on the scene. So engrossed were they in each other that they did not see the fox as he squeezed under the mossed trunk of a windfall to watch them.

Faster and faster ran the doe, and faster Bounce pursued to keep up with her. He made no effort to cut the circle to intercept her, being content to chase without drawing any closer. Presently he barked—three, sharp, terrier-like yaps which carried far through the trees. Then he made one more circuit, tossed his antlered head, and halted. Crossing to the tree he reared on his hind legs and scratched the trunk with his horns, while the doe joined her fawns and stood at gaze. Without any warning, Bounce jumped back from the tree, prancing like a mettle-some hackney, with his slim, polished hooves spurning the sod, and drew up to the doe again.

They repeated the game of running round the tree, and had made perhaps half a dozen circuits when another buck yapped in the wood behind String Lug. Bounce stopped in his tracks, wheeled like a ballet dancer, and walked mincingly towards the sound. As he reached the edge of the clearing the other buck came into view, and String Lug saw the beginning of a fight.

Bounce charged the intruder, met him head on with a crash and rattle of antlers, then danced back, prancing

64

STRING LUG SAW THE BEGINNING OF A FIGHT

and pirouetting, getting ready to repeat the assault. But the newcomer did not stay to argue after the first shock. He was a young beast, short of weight and weapons, getting along on his nerve. Away he went through the trees in long, graceful bounds, barking each time his hooves touched the ground, as if the sound was being knocked out of him by the jolt of each landing. String Lug was indiscreet enough to show himself when he craned his neck to look after him, and Bounce saw him before he had time to get back under cover.

Now, at any other time Bounce would have given all foxes plenty of room—on principle. But this was the rutting season, the season of fighting. His blood was on fire, his brain in a fever, and his discretion asleep. In the fox he saw not only another intruder on his love-making, but a possible menace to the fawns. And maybe he just felt downright cantankerous. In any case, he charged at String Lug, who immediately bolted because he had really nothing to quarrel about.

Emboldened by his easy victory over the other buck and by String Lug's instant retreat, Bounce actually pursued the fox through the length of Blackcraigs, barking as he did so. But String Lug had had enough of being chased. Furthermore, he was just reaching the age when he objected to being pushed about. He was not running from Bounce because he was afraid of him, although he realized that the little buck could be a very dangerous opponent.

Darting into a thicket, he waited till Bounce came up. The buck had now slowed down almost to a walk. The rage was gone from him, and it is probable he had even forgotten what it was he had been chasing. He was rudely reminded of it when String Lug whisked from his ambush like a streak of russet and nipped both his back fetlocks. Bounce wheeled to face his assailant, but somehow the fox was behind him again, nipping him in exactly the same place as before. Bounce's courage deserted him completely, and it was now his turn to flee. He bounded away in twelve-feet jumps, imagining the fox was at his heels. But String Lug, after chasing him for a few yards, gave up. He had no desire for exercise when there was no food at the end of it, and no inclination to start a serious fight over a matter of hurt pride.

The corn, dry and crisp, was stooked, and rustled like the rubbed wings of a dragon-fly when the wind breathed through it. And, suddenly, there was much activity and noise in the fields around Brockhurst. Daily, String Lug heard the laughter and loud voices of men; the stamping and snorting of sweating, heaving horses; and the clang and jangle of machinery. Rooks, white-faced and quizzical, congregated in the stubbles with much swagger and waggle—bright-eyed freebooters with dirt-caked beaks and coats which glinted violet in the sunshine. Down from the moor came the gulls to join them, and soon the first fieldfares and redwings from the far north were chattering in the rowans and elders as their forebears had done every autumn for countless generations.

In the misty sunrise cushats came to feed on the stooks in the cornfield, gobbling a hundred grains for every one devoured by mice, and twenty for every one spoiled by rats. Partridges jugged in the stubble, feeding there when the earth steamed in the morning sun, and in the root fields in the late afternoon. String Lug found their roosting places, where they slept in a semicircle, shoulder to shoulder and head to wind, and tried to stalk them on three nights when no moon shone. He walked up on to them like a pointer dog, but they rose each time with startled *ark-ark-ark* and whirred away in the darkness. Then they changed their roosting place.

But he found them again two nights later, close by a thorn hedge among vetch and clover, where a brown hare passed twice daily on his way to the purple swedes in the next field. String Lug now knew where he had erred before—he had used his scenting powers to judge the distance of his quarry, without using his wet nose to get a dead line on them from the feel of the wind. And that night he killed, because he had solved the problem of distance and direction.

On the day when the first grouse was shot on the moor he trotted down the hedgerow as the sun turned to smoky crimson and swelled to thrice its afternoon size. From a stook ahead of him nineteen cushats—pink-washed silver and hyacinth blue—rose in ragged array, with much wing-slapping, and disappeared in the fire of the sunset. String Lug nosed round the stook, and grinned as he savoured the heavy smell of the birds. He tasted, and spat out, cushat droppings, then left with teeth chittering and mouth watering. This was the third time he had flushed cushats from stooks, and in his brain an idea was born.

Hunting for two hours after darkness fell, he caught only a tiny shrew, and went to bed hungry, fur wet with dew and ears itching with dry seeds of cocksfoot picked up as he poked into hedge bottoms. When he woke up he remembered his plan of the night before and set out for the cornfield, while the sky was still dark as mole's fur and the stars winked icily. Crawling under a stook of eight sheaves as the first pearly tints appeared in the east, he squatted on his belly with his snout screened by the stiff, yellow, dew-shiny corn stalks. A corn husk lodged in the corner of his right eye and irritated so much that he had to risk movement to rub it out with his paw.

Keewick, crossing the cornfield, called out his name as he headed for his roost in Mossrigg, and the first flush of rose heralded the rising sun. The star which had pulsed with green light above Brockhurst all night silvered and vanished, and the cushats came out from the woods to feed.

Eleven of them settled on the stook beneath which String Lug crouched, and started to rip off ears with expert yellow and vermilion beaks. Wariest of birds, they had no suspicion of danger. Presently one of them flew to earth to pick up fallen ears, and for a moment stood framed in the dark triangle which the sloping sheaves formed with the ground. In that instant String Lug struck. And when he burst out from the awry stook he held a flapping cushat in his jaws. He bit it through the keel while the others, skimming the stubble, fled swift and straight for the woods.

This was good hunting—but it could not last; for two reasons. Cushats soon become suspicious of ambush; and stooks do not stand in fields for ever. But the stooks were carted into the Hackamore stackyard before the cushats became alert enough to force String Lug to try other game, and he killed four of them before his cover disappeared.

# Chapter Six

## TRAP-WISE

*I*N THE FIRST WEEK OF NOVEMBER, WHEN GULLS OF three kinds, hungry and clamorous, thronged the brown furrows, String Lug enlarged a rabbit burrow in Mossrigg Strip a stone's-throw from the earth where he was born.

At seven months old, he was a big-boned, handsome fox, not quite set or filled out, but far and away the best-grown of that season's cubs. If he was redder in the coat than his father, he already had the grey mask, the greyish fur on shoulders and withers, and the cloudiness in his brush which betrayed his breeding. In sunlight his flanks were quite russet; but in a company of really red foxes anyone would have called him grey. His stature, length of limb, and depth of flank—apart altogether from his colour—bore testimony to his origin, marking him as the descendant of a race which is to the foxes of England as the lordly peregrine falcon of the Highland crags is to the drab, lack-lustre kestrel in a mews. . . .

Not only in stature had he grown. Wisdom had kept pace with the development of bone and muscle. He had learned the lesson of every experience, and stored the knowledge gained. He knew every ditch, water crossing and runway, every fence, dyke and burrow on his range. And he knew every dog at every farm. Single dogs he feared not, though he always bolted when chased. Yet, time and again, when he saw Jock Simpson with Corrie, he bristled and curled his lip, and longed to meet the shaggy Cairn in the woods alone.

He had come to realize that lights at farms meant men active somewhere. He knew that all men were potentially dangerous and that men with guns were deadly. And he had learned all the supplementary indications of danger. When pigeons, pheasants or partridges flew at night he knew that they had been disturbed; and he always assumed that men were the intruders. The scolding of a magpie or jackdaw, the sight of a fleeing hare, roe deer bounding through a wood at speed, rabbits moving in from the fields in a body—he learned to interpret them all, always exaggerating their significance till his nose had time to test his judgment.

He now moved about with the confident air of one who knows exactly where he is going. He liked travelling by favourite trails and to a regular time-table—so long as it suited his purpose and was safe to do so. For he never became hidebound by the habit, like the hare and the rabbit, or even Bounce. At the slightest indication of anything unusual, at the merest hint of danger, he would change his entire plans and routine. All of which prompted Jock Simpson to say one day to Gallacher: "That fox'll leeve tae scratch an auld heid. If there's a blade o' grass missin' onywhere, he back tracks and does a world tour." For Jock already knew much about String Lug's movements. . . .

For a fortnight after he denned up in Mossrigg String Lug fed mostly on rabbits which he caught among the whins across the burn. Sometimes he ambushed them; sometimes he ran them down. When he was hunting the whins he invariably crossed the burn by using a flat boulder in midstream as a stepping-stone. Like all foxes, he hated getting his feet wet unnecessarily, or unless he chose to wet them. Going out, or coming in, he used the boulder, till it became a habit with him—as far as anything can be called a habit among his kind.

In the same way he developed a special liking for a particular rowan which lay aslant the ridge two hundred yards from his den. He used it for soiling, and never passed it at any time without stopping to sniff it all over as though it held some peculiar and irresistible fascination for him.

Towards the end of the month most of the trees were almost completely bare, grey skeletons stripped of their autumn finery by driving rain and high winds. Here and there golden-brown tatters still clung to the grey and purple branches of the beeches; and some of the birches, in the sheltered rides, were still ribboned with copper and crimson leaves. Dog-roses, aflame with scarlet hips and velvet-tufted with robin's pincushion, clung tenaciously to odd wisps of transparent, water-washed lemon and saffron. Only the stubborn elders and hawthorns had leaves in any quantity, rusting and yellowing leaves which the birds shook loose every time they pulled at elder-berries or sheenless crimson haws.

String Lug had much time in which he had little to do. With hunting good and the nights long, he slept much during the darkness, and was seldom tired during the hours of daylight. So he took to prowling about when the sun was low in east or west. Some days he stalked Brush-tail when the squirrel was on the ground burying nuts which he would soon forget all about. Then Brushtail went to bed for several days during a cold snap and he had to find other amusement.

One chill, frosty morning, when the sky was bright blue and the east a sun-drenched haze, he found sport which satisfied a grudge he had nursed in his heart since he was a cub in Mossrigg. In Laverock Knowe he caught a wounded cock pheasant, resplendent in all the glory of his November plumage. The bird had travelled from beyond Summerfield, escaping because the spaniel sent out after him had preferred to chase rabbits instead of sticking to his blood line. String Lug trotted from the wood with his prize, with the long, barred, golden tail sweeping over his shoulder. As he came into the open a magpie chattered in a beech tree, and stabbed his perch with his ebony beak.

String Lug halted suspiciously, and stood rigid. Still the magpie scolded. His harsh, staccato cackle signified rage and hate, which he vented by gouging bark from his perch with his beak. String Lug read the signs and took two paces forward. The magpie's bright eyes glinted when he saw the fox. With a parting yatter of still more lurid abuse, he danced from his perch and swept over the trees, with spear tail fanned and neck feathers raised.

After a very careful sifting of the air, String Lug could smell only one thing—cat! He peered up and down the woodside. Sure enough there was a half-grown black-and-white kitten eighty fox strides away. She was in the field, playing with a still live vole she had just caught among the blaeberries inside the wood. The kitten's whole attention was taken up with the vole, which she allowed to scurry hither and thither for short distances before scooping it in again with deft sweeps of her paw. Periodically, she rolled over on her back, and held the vole aloft with all her four feet. Her victim's flanks were palpitating. Its fur was soaked and tongue-rubbed, and there was a film over its eyes.

String Lug bristled at sight of the cat and flattened to the ground. His heart thumped with the excitement born of his fury, and he lay perfectly still till he had gained complete control of himself. Laying down his pheasant, he started to crawl towards the kitten, leaving the trail of his passage on the rimed grass. Every faculty was concentrated on the cat. He wanted it more than anything he had ever hunted. And he felt certain he was going to catch it.

He got within twenty yards of the cat before she even stopped playing to look up. As she looked up, with her white-splashed face wrinkled superciliously in question, String Lug jumped into action. As she started to bolt he was already in his stride. Ere she could reach the first oak tree, towards which she whisked for safety, he was upon her, reaching down for her as a greyhound reaches for a hare.

The kitten hissed and wailed as he gripped her. One paw reached up in a lightning stroke when he chopped, the claws hooking in his muzzle as he broke her back. Three times his ivory teeth went *click-click-click*. He tossed the leaping, squirming body aside and watched it go through grotesque acrobatics till it finally stretched out limp on the frost-filmed grass. Then he pawed at the tiny, crimson bubbles which blistered from his muzzle where the cat's claws had struck. The punctures smarted, but String Lug was too elated to heed them.

Before going back for his pheasant, he rolled on the body of the cat several times in a kind of ecstasy. It was the first time he had killed out of sheer vindictiveness.

Trotting back to Mossrigg, he left his pheasant in his burrow and went down to the burn to drink. Near the half-acre fir planting the damp earth was dotted with fungi—agaric and puffball and stinkhorn. A heavy odour was being distilled on the clammy air, the cloying odour of decay. String Lug broke up agaric and puffball with his paw, but sniffed with no sign of distaste at the sickly smell of the frosty white stinkhorns.

A dipper flew from his boulder stepping-stone as he reached the burn lip, and shot downstream like an arrow, calling *chit-chit*. A grey wagtail, black-throated and sulphur-bellied, shrilled *zee-zee-zee-zee* as it skipped airily across pebbles with flirting tail. String Lug jumped on to the boulder as a pair of mallard splashed from the burn and swung heavily into the air. He watched them out of sight and leaped lightly on to the opposite bank. The sere grass below the fence was flat and rasping, but String Lug found cover behind a clump of tall docks with great brown seed heads.

In the pasture fed rooks, jackdaws, cushats and peewits, with three magpies to keep the gathering lively. In the whins beyond, rabbits were squatting unconcernedly, but String Lug knew they would tumble underground the instant the birds rose. And rise they would as soon as he showed himself. So he drew back and worked down the burn for a hundred yards. Again he peered through the fence. Twenty yards away a rabbit sat washing its face with earth-stained forepaws.

Now, String Lug was not hungry. And besides the pheasant in his burrow he had a rabbit buried in Laverock Knowe. But he was fresh, cantankerous and in a mood to hunt for the fun of it. He burst into the pasture without the slightest effort at concealment, and covered perhaps ten paces before the rabbit shot away with ears flat and white fud flashing. String Lug realized he might not catch it before it reached the whins, but he did know which way it would run, which was something. It allowed him freedom to chase at full stretch without having to guard against a sudden side slip or double back on the part of his quarry.

With half the distance covered, he knew he would not catch up with it, but he carried on without slackening pace. He saw the rabbits sitting round the whins pop underground. The birds in the pasture rose in a ragged throng, cawing, yelping and clacking. The pigeons flew straight for the trees, but the rooks swooped down on the coursing fox on ragged wings, followed by several jackdaws. String Lug ignored his noisy escort till he saw the rabbit dart into a burrow mouth. As he turned on his tormentors he was conscious of a faint *click*, which he heard above the raucous calling of the birds. The rabbit suddenly started bobbing up and down outside its burrow. Then it started to squeal.

This was a new development, and String Lug raced to the burrow to collect this very accommodating rabbit which gave up on its doorstep with a twenty yards' lead. The rabbit was struggling violently, spurning brown earth and pellets with its hairy hind pads, and rolling its eyes till the pupils almost disappeared. String Lug was on the point of pouncing when he noticed and heard the rattle of the chain attached to the gin which held the rabbit by both forepaws. This was something new. It was the first time he had seen a gin. He recoiled with head askew and nose twitching.

As he stepped back to figure the matter out a rook slapped him across the face with its wing. The stiff webs of the flight feathers stung him and he jumped at the bird, snarling and clashing his teeth. It wafted up with a startled *caw*. So close did he get to it that he saw its flesh-coloured tongue shoot forward and fall back as it called, and had time to notice the fragment of dried earthworm adhering to its earth-crusted beak. He girned and chopped at the birds till they drifted away to harry a heron which appeared over the trees. The big, slow-winged bird sheered away from his nimble attackers with an astonished *quask-quask*, and disappeared over Mossrigg, taking the circus with him.

String Lug returned to his puzzle. Some foxes learn about gins from their parents; some seem to know about them instinctively; but String Lug was starting from scratch.

He guessed instantly that the rattling chain had something to do with the rabbit's plight, but he couldn't quite figure it. He puzzled hard, sitting quite still, watching, eager to solve the mystery, but content to wait for the answer. Already in his brain the realization was dawning that if the gin could hurt the rabbit it could do the same to him. So he sat on, awaiting developments, having plenty of time on his hands and patience enough to tire a heron.

The rabbit kicked itself into exhaustion and lay, earth-soiled and dishevelled, in the burrow mouth. Its cleft lip was drawn up from its long, yellow incisors. Particles of loose earth adhered to the whites of its eyes, which were already bloodshot. String Lug edged closer at caterpillar pace, with every muscle taut and every sense alert. The rabbit lay still. Tentatively, he reached out with his left paw and touched it. It wriggled slightly, rolling its eyes. String Lug started to push it about with his paw, and finally noticed the jaws of the gin closed on its forelegs.

Again he drew back, while yellowhammers and finches gathered in the drab whins to watch him. He had the answer now. But he was not yet ready to snatch the rabbit. He circled to the top of the burrow, squatted on his belly and reached down with a paw. After pushing the rabbit over and over for a few minutes, he sat down, with brush curled round his haunches, and considered the matter again. Satisfied at last that there was no danger to himself, he leaped nimbly to the bottom side of the burrow, turned, hesitated, then picked up the rabbit.

Of course the gin was anchored, so that he had to tug hard at it to pull it clear. Laying down his burden, he sniffed at the gin, pondering long and critically over the smell of steel. Then he killed the rabbit. He spat out fluffs of blue-grey down, sneezed, reflected, and started to nose round the other burrows. At three holes he discovered gins, recognizing them by the smell of steel which he had just learned. They were all lightly covered over with earth, and only the plates showing. String Lug pawed once at the third hole, very gingerly, but did not investigate further. He knew now what gins could do. . . .

Pica, the magpie, scolded suddenly from a burnside elm, and two cushats swept out in swift, down-curved flight from the next tree. String Lug did not tarry to investigate the cause of the disturbance, but skulked through the whins and into the wood beyond, carrying rabbit and gin without apparent effort.

Near the road he saw Bounce and a doe running the inside of the dyke, without haste, and inferred they had been disturbed in Mossrigg. String Lug chewed the rabbit from the gin, leaving two paws in the jaws, and buried his prize securely. An hour later he trotted back to his den, travelling upwind with his nose asking questions because he knew that two birds and two roe were not fleeing from mice. Man scent tainted the ground near the burn, but was not in evidence anywhere near his burrow, so he went to bed satisfied that the man's passing was of no special significance.

String Lug ate the breast of his pheasant and fell asleep about the time Pate Tamson was cursing the loss of a trap and a rabbit as he sat talking to Gallacher in the Mossrigg Farm kitchen. Pate blamed his old enemy Greyface for the theft. Gallacher was in shirt-sleeves, being impervious to the cold, and was wearing heavy, dung-caked boots and drainpipe trousers. He rubbed his hand reflectively over the two days' bristle on his face.

"The auld grey dug!" he exclaimed, and his eyes twinkled under their bushy overhang. "That's funny. Jock's just efter tellin' me that the grey dug was shote day before yesterday away ayont Laverock Knowe. He must be back fae the deid!"

Pate stared blankly for a moment, then realized Gallacher was serious. He swore. "This must be anither wan. Is Jock richt sure?"

"Go an' ask him," said Gallacher, and his great booming laugh huffed Pate. "He's doon at the tattie pits wi' Andrew and somebody fae the toon, drivin' stabs for fences. Mebbe he was mistook."

Jock Simpson confirmed what Gallacher had already told him. Greyface had been shot by Sinclair in the birch thicket east of Laverock Knowe, and the fox's skin had already been handed over to the town museum for mounting as an exhibit of local interest. Jock was

77

interested in the new development, and Pate gladly poured out the story.

"Where'd ye lose the rabbit?" Jock asked him.

"In the Mossrigg whins, on the burn side o' the knowe. D'ye think it could be a dug?"

"Could be." Jock lit his pipe. "But there's a fox been joukin' aboot the Strip lately, the wan Satan tasted. Damned thing is he buzzes aboot the place like a blue-bottle. He's been in every wid in the place. Ha'e ye ony traps that wid take a fox? I think ye micht . . ."

"I ha'e twa. But at this time o' year, where are ye tae set . . ."

Jock interrupted him.

"Look," he said, and already there was a puckish glint in his grey eyes. "Ye can try this yoursel, but coont me oot in the meantime. There's a flat stane in the burn at Mossrigg that this beast uses reglar. Set wan there if ye like. But ye'll need tae hide it weel. This beast has a mind for detail and he'll ken the smell o' steel by this time. Make nae mistake aboot that. But ye can see how ye get on."

"Mebbe this was just an accidental thing?" said Pate.

"Hope springs eternal," laughed Jock. Then banter-ingly: "He'll be back!"

Pate had to leave it at that. He could never understand the fencer's indulgent attitude to foxes. For a week he did nothing with traps, confining himself to snaring, in the hope that the fox would move on or forget. String Lug, visiting the whins daily, discovered no hidden gins, nor did he find the smell of steel at any burrow on his range. So he took to watching Pate as he went his rounds setting snares, and in due course discovered rabbits in them.

Pate found the first of his emptied snares hanging kinked and twisted from a fence wire, with wisps of rabbit fluff scattered round about. He guessed the culprit at once, and marvelled at the identical technique of the two foxes, for String Lug had not spent any time on the snare or peg. Like Greyface he had eaten through the neck of the rabbit. In the pub that night, Pate swore terrible vengeance on String Lug, and boasted that he would soon be sending another fox-hide to the taxidermist.

For almost three days String Lug holed up when smirring rain and gusts of cold sleet drenched the woods. The food he had in his burrow saved him from hunting in the cheerless drizzle, so he only got his fur wet when going down to the burn to drink. He hated the clinging mists, the billowing clouds of grey vapour which swept the ground, blotted out the world, and merged earth and sky in one great haze of wetness. Gossamer webs of wet mist tickled his eyebrows every time he looked out of doors and soft, sludgy earth squeezed between his toes at every step. The sodden trees drip-dripped with gleaming trunks. The green moss-furring on the beeches became black and rain-shiny, and pools of water collected in the crotches of the older trees where ferns grew in summertime.

The drip and pour of the rain ceased and the wet woods steamed in the heat of a weak sun. Every pool and puddle mirrored the sky and birds bathed in splashes of azure. A tree-creeper scurried up and down a birch trunk ere the silver bark was dry, and sat on his tail, with eyes staring, when he saw the fox look out on the damp world. String Lug saw the little mousy bird and ignored him. When he started to shake soil from his fur, the tree-creeper flew away in fright, calling *tsee-tsee-tsit* loudly enough to make Pica cock his head and Keewick open his lazy eyes to slits.

Pica chocked and bit twigs as the fox walked down the slope, and Keewick, huddled against his pine trunk, clicked his hooked beak thrice and winked with one lustrous eye. String Lug acknowledged the wink by showing teeth. Keewick shook out a casting, a wet, furry object half the size of a mouse, which rolled down the slope and came to rest against a greening cone as the fox passed under his tree. String Lug sniffed at the casting and walked on at leisurely pace, furious at Pica for sending up the ears of every rabbit across the burn. At the water's edge he stopped to scratch his right ear with his right hind paw. His teeth *click-clicked* as he clawed, and he whined once when his nails bit his ragged ear too deeply.

The burn was high, with low growth awash, and fed by a hundred little rillets which had gouged their way down the slope carrying leaves, twigs and rabbit pellets. String Lug paused on the lip of the burn, forefeet in the swish of water and hindfeet on the bank. He felt vaguely uneasy, yet unable to account for it. For some minutes he stood rigid, with rump above the level of his ears. Then he stepped back to the bank. He scanned the water, upstream and down, the opposite bank, the field beyond, the boulder. . . . The boulder! That was it! It had changed. There was green moss on it now, and grass fibre. And they had certainly not been brought down by the spate, for the boulder top was still inches above the water.

String Lug's uneasiness vanished. But he did not jump on to the boulder. He wanted first of all to investigate the matter of its changed appearance. Wading out to it, shoulder deep, he sniffed critically. Through the odour of the moss, and in spite of the scent-destroying wash of water, he recognized the smell. . . . Steel! String Lug pondered, but did not paw. He gripped the outer fuzz of the moss covering and jerked, sliding back on his haunches till he almost fell in the water. The gin lay exposed, slick on his stepping-stone, with jaws spread to catch his feet.

At that moment String Lug knew fear—real fear. It is doubtful if he realized at once that the gin had been set specially for himself, or that Pate was the man responsible. What he did appreciate was that he might well have walked right into it had he not stopped to consider the boulder's altered appearance. But when he found another

HE GRIPPED THE OUTER FUZZ OF THE MOSS

gin carefully planted beside his favourite rowan tree on the ridge, he knew that it was meant for him. And that was the beginning of trap wisdom for String Lug.

Traps set for the unwary and unsuspecting, in paths well trodden by fearless feet, invariably grip legs in time. A beast which knows the power of traps is more difficult because it has got to be fooled into believing none is planted in its path. But a beast which not only understands traps, but gets around to looking for them everywhere because it realizes its capture is being planned, will break the trapper's heart before it loses a toe.

String Lug broke Pate Tamson's heart and kept all his toes. And Pate stopped boasting about catching him.

# Chapter Seven

## LEAN DAYS

———————

*T*HE FIRST FLURRY OF SNOW CAME ON A MORNING OF glittering blue when the wind blew snell from the east. It was scanty enough, small and fluffy like tit feathers, whisked horizontally across the bare fields so that it webbed with white every hedgerow which crossed its path. The massed gulls in the high Hackamore pasture stood it out till the daylight was an hour old, facing the east with puffed feathers and eyes sunk to the wing elbows. Then they cascaded into the air, an ermine-tipped turmoil of silver wings, and swept away to squabble at the coup on the edge of the town.

At midday the dun clouds rifted and drew away to the south-west, like the nictitating membrane from the eye of a bird, revealing the hard, icy blue pupil of the sky. The snowflakes swirled in handfuls, then twos, then singly, and presently ceased altogether. The sun on its low arc glistened pale gold, but the warmth was sucked out of it by the freezing sky. The wind rose in a succession of shrieking gusts to a steady gale, in which the rusty leaves of the scrub beeches in the hedgerows rasped harshly, and the laced limbs of the big trees creaked and groaned as they rubbed against each other.

In the Mossrigg wheatfield, rooks, cushats and magpies staggered and side-stepped as they fed on the fast-freezing ground. The ragged trousers of the parchment-faced rooks whipped about in the wind, as they delved with much wing-flicking and tail-fanning. Pica was one of sixteen bellicose magpies dibbling in the hardening earth crust, and time and again he was almost toppled forward on to his beak when the wind tipped him under the tail. The pigeons danced in unwilling circles as cupped wings caught the wind. Across the pasture, beyond the fence, sheep plodded in twos and threes to the shelter of the Strip, while the wind combed the wool on their spines into a variety of ephemeral partings.

Snow started falling again in the late afternoon, great florin flakes which lay as they settled, soundless as the folding wings of an owl. The wind died to a light but dead chill breeze. Clouds once more rolled up to hide the sky's vitreous blue. When the sun went down there was no fire in the west to announce its departure.

String Lug stalked from his lair in Mossrigg two hours after sundown, and found himself in a new world—a hushed, lifeless world, smothered under a thick mantle of white. It was a two-colour landscape he saw. Everything which was not white was black as pine tops seen against the moon. String Lug pondered the phenomenon with something akin to awe, with the same amazement as intensively-kept hens which find the colour of their floor litter violently changed. He peered up with crinkled face through the down-swirl, as if hoping to view the full moon which he knew should be there. He pawed the snow and sniffed it, and snatched with his jaws at the falling flakes. His face and eyebrows were soon bushed white with it. He shook himself vigorously when he realized he was wearing a white wrap, and sent the wet, clinging stuff off in a mist and powder spray. Then he returned to his burrow to think.

Lying just inside his burrow he half-closed his eyes and watched the snow-dance, intrigued at the endless pattern of it, at the unpredictable and unrelated behaviour of the goosefeather flakes as they wavered, danced, spiralled, whirled or swept to earth. The noiselessness of the snowfall puzzled him vaguely. Even the merest smir of rain whispers its contact with the earth. But here was no rain whisper, only endless, bewildering movement, silent as owl flight.

String Lug wriggled farther back into his burrow till his snout was clear of the clammy, spider's web touch of the snow flakes. Little beads of water dripped from his whiskers and eyebrows, and his outer fur became damp as the remaining white particles melted. He could see some distance through the trees in spite of the myriad, shuddering discs which blurred his vision. He needed to go out, for all he had in his burrow was the hind half of a rabbit which he had killed that morning after a tiring stalk among threshes in a grubby pasture away beyond Laverock Knowe. But he was not yet certain that he liked the snow, or that he was even prepared to hunt in it. Up to that moment he disliked only two things when he was hunting—high wind and driving rain. The snow was new, and he still had an open mind on the subject.

Those were lean days for String Lug and all the hunting clans. Stoats in winter dress, with black-tipped squirrel tails, filed down from the moor in famished bands, ten to seventeen strong, to ravage the white farmlands. Weasels moused underground. Foxes, with brushes icicled in the gelid night wind, raided hen roosts, and got away with nothing worse than small shot in feet and brisket because farmers shot poorly in the moonshine. Keewick and Tufter, the long-eared owl, hunted the stackyards. Kree, the kestrel from the moor, came down to hunt small birds, for mice were hard to come by. Golden plover and peewits vanished from the fields, and small birds with empty stomachs fell dead from perches.

String Lug had to brave the wind, for there were no still days or nights. He killed rats at Hackamore and Summerfield, and chopped Jock Simpson's game bantam cockerel, which he found roosting on the ground, half covered with drifting snow. The drift covered his tracks, so Jock was never sure what had happened to his bantam.

On the sixth day after the snowfall, when a gold and vermilion chord of the sun still showed above the smoky haze of the horizon, he found the recent trail of a hare in the thin, wind-blown snow of the wheatfield, and followed it. He crossed five fields and the powdered ice of a burn, where the hare's tracks were writ plain for all to see. Near the burn he found a dead redwing which he took time to eat before continuing on the trail of the hare.

Two fields farther on he found boot tracks joining the trail. String Lug noted them carefully, identifying them by the scent lying in them. He had half a mind to give up, but his will to know led him on. He followed very circumspectly now. In the corner of a rough pasture he came upon blood in the snow. The hare, betrayed by his tracks, had been shot as he bounded from his form in a reed clump. So String Lug learned the peril of tracking snow. . . .

It was now into the calling season. Only a thin tracking snow lay on the fields; but the Frost King still held sway, and each morning every bud was iced and every tree white with rime. String Lug heard the first barking of dog foxes between midnight and dawn, when the moon was a silver talon and the stars winked coldly from a sky of velvet. He listened intently to the *yap-yap-yarr* which is the universal call of a dog fox seeking a mate, and knew instantly the significance of the sound.

Next evening he ranged far to the east, five miles beyond Laverock Knowe, in country he knew little about, crossing the trails of three dog foxes without winding a solitary vixen. Reaching the heather fringe an hour before daybreak, he stopped at a wide ditch. String Lug tested the ice which covered six feet of dark, peaty water, and chose to jump rather than walk across. Slipping at the take-off, he got barely a nail grip on the other side and fell sprawling on the ice. Luckily, it was thick enough to stand the shock, and merely creaked instead of breaking, so he climbed out none the worse and shook the ice sweepings from his coat. Shortly afterwards he found a peat and heather butt, fenced on one side with corrugated sheets held by stakes. One side of the butt was caved in. String Lug, sensing its possibilities, looked it over and decided on it as a lie during the next daylight.

Before crawling in, he quartered the surrounding heather like a setter in the hope of snatching a quick breakfast. The moor was patchy white, for the snow barely reached the first joint of the heather, which showed black. On a rise he killed a white stoat as it belly-crawled through the heather tangle. With the prize in his jaws, he travelled twenty paces on his back trail before it occurred to him that the stoat had been in the middle of a stalk when he killed it. He retraced his steps, dropped his stoat, and tested the wind. Nothing. But the stoat might have been doing a cast for cover. String Lug edged across the wind, which soon told him what he wanted to know. The smell was grouse, new to him, but gamey. And instantly he flattened into invisibility.

In six minutes, after a crawl-up noiseless as cat tread, he was in his killing crouch, his nose having marked the exact position of his victim. His rush was swift, accurate, perfectly timed. Three grouse exploded into the air with a burr and tremor of wings, but the fourth was chopped and secure in the fox's jaws before their droppings pattered on the heather. In his eagerness, String Lug bit the head clean off the bird. It fell at his feet as he mouthed for a more comfortable grip on the body. The beak still opened and closed spasmodically and the eyes still blinked. String Lug trotted away with the body, indifferent to its wild flapping or the wild call *go-back, go-back, ho-ack, ho-o-a-ah* which issued from the severed windpipe. Being provident, he went back for the stoat after he had deposited his grouse in the butt.

String Lug spent the following day and night, and the next daylight, on the moor, and wasted half the second darkness following a dog and vixen before he became convinced they were a mated pair. Only when the vixen finally rushed at him, liberally displaying ivory and reaching for his big tendon, did he accept defeat and retire. He dozed through the rest of the moonless night in the butt, then hunted from daybreak till after sunrise without killing. In his lair he ate the tough, rubber-and-whipcord body of the stoat without relish, and spent much time cleaning himself afterwards. During the late afternoon he lay watching ducks and gulls flying overhead, and listening to the crowing of grouse. Not yet did he know of the loch two miles to the south where grey geese, and ducks of many kinds, congregated during the calling season of foxes.

He left when the sun was an orange and crimson smudge in the fumid western sky, and passed through a belt of tall pines into a birch swamp, where he disturbed a roe doe as she browsed standing on her hind legs. The swamp suddenly gave way to dry ground and the birches to a vast beechwood, where each limb's burnished leaves whispered wood scandal to the wind. String Lug nosed critically among the upturned roots of a riven beech where a vixen had squatted and made blood-water some hours before. Faint as the scent was, he could own it, and cast about hopefully but helplessly for her trail. Nor did he find other sign-water in the vicinity.

But the questing fever was on him and he roamed many miles through fields and woods till he reached a planting of young, cobwebby spruce by the railway. He found no vixen, but could hear afar the barking of a dog fox. In the planting he rose a mountain hare which he tried to follow. The young growth slowed him hopelessly and he stopped, while the hare raced for nearly a mile before stopping to take breath. String Lug followed the railway for something like half a mile, stepping from sleeper to sleeper, crossing and re-crossing the track, then slipped down the embankment near a ramshackle steading and killed a rat by the pigsty.

Twice, while the darkness was still young, he heard the squalling of a vixen and was lured many miles without finding the signs he sought. His wanderings brought him back to the beechwood where he had first smelt vixen. He curled up under a bracken-draped windfall just after Orion had completed his scintillating dash across the southern sky, and while the Great Bear lay on his back in a snowdrift cloud which hid his rump.

The morning was raw and String Lug woke with a shudder, despite his thick coat. He clawed his ribboned right ear, to which the skeleton of a beech leaf clung, and shook himself vigorously. He yawned, breathing tenuous vapour, and searched viciously with his teeth for a flea in his armpit. And all at once he wanted to go home. . . .

Once out of the beechwood he travelled at a dog-trot till he reached the road. For some reason he chose to follow the burn and hedges by the roadside instead of cutting across country. He walked the frozen bed of the burn till he came to a gorge, with gouged and fissured whin walls glassed with ice. Here he took to the bank, returning to the burn below a frozen waterfall where otter-tail icicles hung unsparkling in the half light. When the burn forked from the road, he hugged the thorn hedge till he reached a gate fashioned by two birch trunks hanging by rusting chains to rust-eaten hooks. At the gate he halted to watch two men with guns in the field across the road. They were returning to the farm on the slope, after spending eight hours in hen-houses waiting for a fox that had killed birds the night before, but which had hunted elsewhere while they froze and cursed him for not returning to try again.

Round a bend, beside a wood, was another farm with a duckpond opposite the close. The pond was frozen and

ONE SWIFT RUSH TOOK STRING LUG AMONG THEM

twenty-one Aylesbury ducks stood wing-flapping and feather-preening on the ice. One swift rush took String Lug right among them. He snatched and chopped, and twenty ducks scattered in billowing orange-and-white confusion, quarking and craiking their alarm. The twenty-first was carried off in the jaws of a galloping fox. String Lug fled across a grassless half-acre, where pigs the colour of oak apples rooted and guzzled in all but the hardest weather. The half-acre was patchy with snow, and frost hardened in the patterns to which it had been churned by the pigs' feet. String Lug skidded three times on the pitted surface as he crossed with his duck.

In the wood he slowed down to a walk and changed his mouth-hold on the duck. Winding dogs at the cottage of John Long, the gamekeeper, he made a discreet detour. Beside the green-velveted stones of a collapsed drystone dyke he saw the stiff body of a weasel. Nearby was another, newly dead, in a gin. The trapped weasel had been lured to his death by the corpse summons which never fails to attract his kind, and which John Long exploited because somebody had once told him that all weasels should be killed.

The sun's rim was just showing when he reached the wheatfield, having carried a duck five miles at a smarter pace than he usually travelled unladen. Instead of going in to Mossrigg by his favourite route, he held away to the south-west corner so that he could go in against the wind. On the corner was a deep, rushy gully, with a cattle trough, fed by a rusty pipe from a spring. He stopped short of the dyke on the wood edge when he saw Keewick, Pica the magpie, a rook and several tits gossiping in the branches overhead, preoccupied with something on the ground.

The behaviour of the birds, especially Pica, made him curious. He walked slowly forward, dropped his duck, sniffed through a space between stones without showing himself above the dyke top, and smelled—cat. Pica hopped higher, perch stabbing and *chock-tlicking*, when he saw the fox rear on his hind legs to peer over the dyke. Keewick, flying to another tree, swooped as he did so, and String Lug saw movement along the dyke, between twin spikes of gorse. Dropping back on all fours, he moved down the outside of the dyke till he reached a slip-through used by rabbits, where the smell of cat was overpowering.

String Lug leaped lightly on to the glassed top of the dyke, and looked down. In a rabbit snare near the slip-through was a cat, held by a hind leg. It was a great, moon-faced cat, with temendous claws and forepaws, and whiskered like an otter. String Lug jumped down lightly beside it, with his ears flattened and his lips drawn back from his teeth. The cat was Satan. To Satan String Lug was a fox; but to String Lug Satan was more than a cat. He was *the* cat. . . .

The cat, hissing and snarling viciously, fluffed his tail and pulled savagely at the wire. His eyes closed to moist slits as lifted lips revealed his tremendous teeth. String Lug knew why the cat couldn't move, and gloated. He grinned right from ear to ear, a wicked grin, while his narrowed eyes gleamed hate. He sat down on his hunkers and relished the situation. For there was not the slightest shadow of doubt that he recognized the cat, realized its helplessness and was savouring the moment to the full before going in to chop.

Satan tugged more furiously at the snare. The wire had cut his right hind leg clean to the bone, without severing the great tendon. Above and below the noose the flesh was puffed and purple. String Lug, rising, moved in slowly, with his tusks bared to the gums and his brush hanging rigid between his hocks. He started moving round the cat in circles, snapping and pawing at intervals, and going faster and faster on each circuit. Satan turned with him, green-eyed and snarling, never allowing the fox to get behind him.

When String Lug saw him helplessly entangled in the free wire he rushed in, parrying the great cat's armed forepaw deftly with his own. Satan screeched like the brakes of a locomotive as String Lug reached for his back. Click of ivory and the fox danced back, while the cat rolled over, kicking and leaping. Again String Lug cut in, and again his teeth met fleetingly in Satan's spine. And this time he stepped back slowly, for the Mossrigg tom-cat was dead. . . .

# Chapter Eight

## A MATE

***

*O*N A NIGHT OF HEAVY CRANREUCH, WHEN THE black, shaggy heads of the tall Hackamore pines brushed the face of a lop-sided, silver moon, three men and a dog crossed the stubble field from the road and filed silently along the inside of the dyke at Brockhurst. Behind a jumble of whin stones, at a break in the dyke where fireweed flaunted rosy-purple spires in summer, the men sat down, drawing collars over ears and coat tails round knees. The black dog crouched without fuss at their feet.

Jock Simpson pulled the dog's ears as he wriggled his back to get it comfortably bedded against the dyke. His companions were Geordie, the cattleman from Summerfield, and Robert, the village schoolmaster's son. They had joined Jock in the hope of catching a glimpse of a vixen he had seen passing through the gap three nights running.

"This is likely the night she'll go trapsin' somewhere else," observed Jock, who had a long experience of the vagaries of foxes. "Tho' she should come if she hisna been frichted. But ye'll baith need tae sit tighter than a slater under a stane."

The dog, a big-boned, black Labrador bitch, a fourth-season gun-dog with the reputation of never having lost a runner, wagged her otter tail at the sound of her master's voice. Badly scared as a puppy by a crabbed old dog fox, she had never quite got over her fear, and still cringed at the sight or smell of one. Geordie was doubtful about her.

"You should ha'e brocht Corrie," he said.

"An' ha'e him barkin' and chasin' ower half the parish

in the middle o' the nicht! This is nae time for terriers. The bitch is maybe scared, but she'll gi'e us plenty warnin' if there's a beast in the wind, withoot tellin' the world an' his wife we're here."

Comfortably warm at the beginning of their vigil, the clammy, frosty air ate into them before half an hour dragged by. The silence of the wood hissed unceasingly in their ears. The moon sailed behind a cloud and the lights went off in Brockhurst. The treetops shuddered in a momentary breeze. The rattle of a stone up the woodside betrayed a rabbit bobbing over the dyke as it came in from the fields. Then from away up the field came the scream of a vixen—a harsh, mournful, rending cry, which made Robert's neck hairs tingle. When the moon came out of hiding they saw her on the headrigg, a formless smudge against the hoar.

The dog quivered and Jock whispered: "Here she comes. If she keeps her direction she'll come nearer than twenty yairds afore she winds us."

Silence for a minute. Then a dog fox barked in Brockhurst. Jock cut short the queries of the others with a sharp "Wheesht!" and pointed far up the field to the dog fox who was trotting out to meet the vixen. They watched him go up to her and run back again. He repeated the performance four times while the vixen came on steadily towards the gap in the dyke.

At that moment String Lug crossed the frost-jewelled road from Summerfield into Brockhurst. Tufter, the long-eared owl, swooped between trees as he glided over the dyke. He nosed round the right angle formed by it and the long dyke behind which the men were sitting, and jumped into the field. His pace was slow, for he was leg-weary. In a fortnight of feverish questing for a mate he had lost appetite and weight, but had gained in toughness and resolution after many cut-and-run fights with older foxes who found him no easy opponent.

The night being almost windless, he walked within gunshot of the men before he scented them. His nose plotted their exact position after much testing of the air, and he drew in against the dyke. Whether he saw the foxes in the field is open to question. Suddenly he barked, three short, harsh barks which halted the wooers and brought exclamations from the hidden men. They all looked round, and Jock Simpson whispered: "That's lousin' time. We're rumbled. . . ."

String Lug stepped back twenty paces and barked again. Then he slithered over the dyke into the moonlit gloom of the wood, and edged cautiously into the tree cover. Jock saw the twin firepoints of his eyes as he looked round once. Three more barks and they saw or heard him no more. The foxes in the field, with ears up and noses uneasy because they could not get answers to their questions, parted company. The men rose in time to see the dog fox disappear over the headrigg and the vixen race with flying brush to the cattle-trough corner of Brockhurst.

In the tangy, powdery gloom among the pines String Lug stood—listening. He heard the men cross the road into Summerfield, and presently cushats flashed overhead on whistling wings to confirm his judgment. After a lapse of a minute, in which he licked the fur of his chest, he skulked cautiously back to the dyke and jumped into the stubble as another cloud hid the moon. He crossed the outgoing trail of the men as Keewick hooted above his head. The owl had killed two rats in Hackamore Farm and was on his way home to sleep till the next twilight. Ere he reached his roost in Mossrigg, String Lug had found the spot where the foxes had parted company. After much sibilant sniffing, he left and ran the vixen's line to the cattle-trough corner, with mouth watering and teeth chittering.

At the cattle trough he stopped to lick ice before

continuing on the vixen's trail. Rounding the dyke corner, he reached a hollow where the wind had blown the snow to hock depth, and nosed at a nebulous, paw-sized softness in the frost-glazed surface. String Lug did not linger at the vixen's sign, but hurriedly followed her trail to where she had climbed the dyke into the wood. Going over right in her tracks, he jumped well out to clear bramble tendrils on the inside. On the edge of the trees he froze in mid-stride. Slowly his birses rose, and with a sideways tilt of his head he bared his teeth.

Right in his path a dog fox was sniffing and tongueing the vixen's tracks. The fox was a beast called The Limper, big, red, with one short leg, and at that time three years old. He was a moor fox, from the high ground to the east. He had already lost his mate on the moor by poisoning and was down in the wooded country seeking another. The Limper hated all foxes—except vixens in the running season—and was in no mood for interference. String Lug would have passed quietly, for he knew the vixen was not far away. But The Limper knew it too, and had no intention of allowing any fox ahead of him. Without warning he rushed at String Lug, with teeth showing and tail flexed for swiping. String Lug did not yield. He was as big as The Limper, as tough and powerful, and in no mood to be hustled. And he had learned a great deal in two weeks of brawling. . . .

As The Limper lashed out with his brush, String Lug sidestepped and closed, and ripped his jowl with one raking slash of tusks. It was a perfectly delivered cut-and-run thrust, in approved fox fashion, and he was round behind The Limper before the first drops of blood stained the snow. The sudden shock and pain stung The Limper to white-hot fury. He was an old campaigner, used to coming out on top in duels, and didn't like having his jaw opened. But his self-confidence had received a jolt. It received a still greater jolt when String Lug whacked

95

him across the eyes with his frost-gritty brush. As he staggered back, almost in a panic, he heard the click of his opponent's teeth dangerously near his big tendon.

Jerking away his leg, like a cat whipping a paw from water, he skidded and fell in his own gore. Like a flash, String Lug was in, nipped the pads of his forefeet, jumped right over him, wheeled, and again raked his face before he could scramble to his feet. At that The Limper lost heart. His courage melted. He wanted to be clear of it all without any more holes in his hide. Shaken, and in a panic, he staggered away, cowed by a demon who fought with experience beyond his age.

String Lug licked his right shoulder where The Limper's teeth had loosened fur, and trotted into the trees, ears up, tongue a-loll and tail carried gay. He passed through gloomy hollows and lanes of moonlight, where the air was tangy and cold, and black, down-clutching skeleton branches of firs clawed at his fur. A low-roosting pheasant *cu-cu-cupped* twice in drowsy query when he squeezed through the rhododendron thicket into the big ride between Brockhurst and Blackcraigs. There he found the vixen, standing against the trunk of a wire-bitten sycamore, scraping at the curling bark with her forepaws.

The vixen was two years old, slim, red, and smaller than String Lug. She knew she was being followed and was expecting him. For some reason, she showed no desire to bite; indeed, she accepted him right away, without flattening her ears. They touched noses, sniffed each other critically, head to toes and back to front, and settled everything on the spot. String Lug washed her ears with his warm tongue, to which caress she submitted luxuriously with uptilted snout and half-closed eyes. Only when he tried to rush things did she jump away and uncover the tips of her tusks in warning.

They loped along the ride together, the vixen in front and String Lug with his nose at her flank. It was gleaming in the ride, the moon's rays being baffled by the tall trees on the rise. A weasel, red-eyed and snarling without chatter, watched them from a dyke cranny as they climbed the ridge into Mossrigg. Neither String Lug nor his mate paid any heed to the snarler. His back was in the cranny, and they knew the rest of him would follow before they could take two strides in his direction. They might have gone back had they known he had a cushat under the mossed whinstones, a piner he had found ground-flapping on the slope not long before.

Both foxes were hungry: String Lug especially so. For three days he had eaten only morsels, being stomach-heavy with the fever of questing. He wanted to hunt rabbits in the whins across the burn, or go rat-killing; but he couldn't induce the vixen to follow him. He led her to his lair, prepared to surrender it to her, but when she came out backwards, after the briefest examination, she turned and nipped his ear to show her disapproval. String Lug sat down and grinned. When she came up to him he reached out to bite playfully at her forepaws. In return, she bit the loose skin of his cheek; but it was not playful. It hurt.

String Lug followed the vixen down to the burn. A waterhen, preening as she stood on the decayed cushion of a sedge clump, at the mouth of a deep ditch draining into the burn, called *krurr-k: krurr-k* to her mate in the field on the other side. String Lug stopped to weigh chances, but the vixen pushed on, without even an upward glance when the birds rose clumsily and flew *krooking* and *tut-tutting* in alarm. The waterhens flew downstream, turned left at the bridge below Mossrigg Farm, circled field and whins, and pitched at their starting point. String Lug, with left ear up and head cocked, hesitated for a moment, but followed the vixen without fuss.

The foxes followed the burn to the bridge. They ducked under the bottom wire of the fence and crossed the road, over frozen puddles where the ice lay shattered and splintered by the wheels of farm carts. Following the burn again, hugging the bank where alders grew thick, and running the water edge where there were no trees to hide them, they reached a wide loop where drain pipes lay piled on the flat bank top. The burn forked at this point, on its way through rich arable land and round netted plantings to join the greater water at the railway bridge three-quarters of a mile away. Here the foxes crossed, passing over a great, sloping field under winter wheat, and skirting a belt of trees at the headrigg. Following a long hedgerow, they soon reached the low dyke at the kitchen garden of Laverock Knowe Farm.

Having been to Laverock Knowe before, the vixen knew her way about. What she didn't know was that she was expected. Davidson slept that night with loaded shotgun standing against the wall by his bedroom window. His collie bitch, nursing five puppies, had been moved to a chicken house nearer the cart-shed where a dozen white hens roosted because they couldn't be persuaded to go elsewhere. It was in the cart-shed that the vixen had killed birds two nights before.

Now that he was on the spot String Lug joined actively in the raid, though with less zest than he showed for other forms of hunting. At the cart-shed he stopped playing tailpiece and took the initiative. A fat Wyandotte hen, perched on the tip of a plough handle, squawked once and died, flapping headless in expert jaws. As the vixen, mounting the driving seat of the horse-rake, snatched at a beefy cockerel on the V-bar between the shafts, the other hens cackled and shuffled till slipping feet started wings clapping to add to the uproar. The collie barked furiously —if tardily—and the foxes heard the rattle of claws on wood as she jumped at the door of the chicken house.

The white cockerel, with blood spurting from his neck, was pulled from his perch. A window opened with a screak as the vixen jumped down with her heavy burden. Glitter of gun barrels in the weak moonshine and String Lug flashed behind the shed as Davidson's twelve-bore belched flame, smoke and No. 3 shot. Pellets tinkled on metal and spurted frozen snow in the vixen's face. She got away with one pellet in her leg, for Davidson had shot too low: but she had to go without seven and a half pounds of Wyandotte cockerel.

String Lug skulked across the frost-skinned causeway stones of the farm close, and passed into a field through an open gate. Every hoof-mark at the gate was lidded with wafer ice. He didn't stop running till he reached the road above the glen of Laverock Knowe wood. The vixen met him two minutes later, and in two seconds took possession of the headless hen. Becoming tail-piece again, String Lug followed her into the glen without protest. Below a bulging scaur of whin, feathered with ice, she turned and warned him off, while keeping her grip on the hen. She disappeared into a hole at the bottom of the rock wall, and clicked her teeth without savagery when he tried to follow her. So he took the hint and left.

Before the vixen had eaten her fill of hen, he was rolling ecstatically on the body of Satan in Brockhurst. The dead cat, with the snare still entangled, had been thrown aside by Pate Tamson. Beyond swearing at a ruined snare, he had thought nothing about it, assuming the cat had killed himself struggling. String Lug had gone through the ritual of rolling on the cat almost nightly since he killed him, especially after losing a fox fight, when the act relieved his feelings mightily.

He left Brockhurst with little cat smell on him, for the carcase was sealed by frost and could not have been smelt by a downwind fox at thirty paces. At the burn he stalked, and caught, one of the waterhens he had hankered for earlier in the night, and ate it on the spot. On his way back to Laverock Knowe he rose a hare in the wheatfield and coursed it right to the wood, where he lost it. He lost it because he could not stand the pace, being belly-heavy with the waterhen he had just eaten. Poking his nose into the hole below the scaur he found the vixen still there, and curled up nearby to doze till she came out.

For the next week he was tied to Laverock Knowe. The vixen would not forsake her own den. String Lug slept at the pad-worn mouth of an old rabbit burrow under a stump, after scraping away matted leaves till the size suited him. They hunted together during the early part of each night, then went their own ways till the next dusk. The vixen had a failing for poultry, and they raided three farms in six nights, their best slaughter being seven pullets roosting in a house with a pophole big enough to admit a pig. But they left Laverock Knowe Farm severely alone.

The thaw came with a raw wind from the west, but the sparse snow when it melted drained hardly a trickle into the burns and ditches. At dawn on a Sunday morning, when the elder buds were rupturing, String Lug led his mate to the cattle-trough corner at Brockhurst. Mated, she was less self-willed, and followed him quietly. He was taking her to share with him the luxury of a roll on the body of Satan. The weather being soft, with a Scotch mist damping the foxes' fur, the stench of the cat was heavy on the air, and the vixen winded it while she was yet some distance from the wood.

Together they slithered over the dyke, feet printing the soft ground as they landed. Side by side, they approached the cat. String Lug savoured the odour with relish, but did not run right up to the cat. He was puzzled by the presence of three scatterings of dead leaves and teased-out pine needles, neatly arranged round the body, which were not there the previous day. He moved forward suspiciously, with his nose down seeking answers. Then he smelt it—steel! There was not the slightest whiff of man, but steel!

He snarled a warning at the vixen and gnashed his teeth in her face. But she brushed past him, chopping, and walked right on to a leaf circle. A sudden *click*, and a simultaneous pain in her foot, and she jumped back with a girning snarl, dragging a heavy gin on her paw. She pulled and squirmed and bit at the metal till her gums bled and she broke a tusk. String Lug snaked behind her in a frenzy. He could not get near her, for she reached at him with slavering jaws whenever he snatched at the gin. The pain in her wrist was excruciating, but try as she might, she could not free herself, nor break the gin from its anchor. And then, while String Lug whined at her back, she sprung another of the hidden terrors, and was gripped by the tip of her brush.

Lying spreadeagled, with flanks heaving and jaws dripping blood and saliva, she allowed String Lug to approach her. Her wrist was already swollen above the grip of the steel teeth. String Lug, knowing what could and could not be done about gins, started to bite at her wrist. The fresh stab of pain stung her and she raked his face; but, presently, as if realizing she could never hope to help herself, she allowed him to work without even looking at him. She lay mute, but panting, as he chewed at bone and sinew. But he was interrupted before he had quite severed her paw.

Over the dyke came Jock Simpson, followed by Pate Tamson with his .22 smooth-bore in his hand. String Lug fled, dishevelled and snarling, giving Pate no chance to fire at him. The moocher cursed at missing a shot, but grinned when he saw the trapped vixen.

"Ye were right, Jock," he said. "But how did ye tumble tae foxes?"

"Even foxes leave tracks," replied Jock quietly. "Best put a bullet in her heid, quick," and he nodded at the vixen. "A blin' man could ha'e seen a fox killed the cat, an' how ye didna see he was rollin' on it reglar bates me!"

Pate shot the vixen, and ended her pain. Then he undid the gins.

"This'll be the snare specialist, eh?"

Jock scratched his head reflectively. "Man, I widna be share. Maist likely it's the wan that got awa."

Not long after they left they heard the pitiful wailing of a fox and stopped to listen. And when they moved on again, long afterwards, String Lug was still mourning the loss of his mate.

# Chapter Nine

———————————

*T*HE SWALLOWS CAME WHEN BOUNCE WAS STILL IN velvet, and before the first of the year's fox cubs had opened their eyes in nurseries dark as their former blindness. Woodcock, fast-flying on slow wings, roded each sunset at tree height, in owl-like flight, croaking as they circled on the same route each night. When the woodcock started their eve flight in Hackamore a cock pheasant, in jewelled plumage, crowed and drummed noisily, standing on tiptoe with puffed-out chest. At these signs of darkening, Keewick, with a mate and five owlets in a pine tree, winked slyly and hooted his acknowledgement of the time signal.

The days were close and drizzly, with flashes of golden sunshine, when the thorn hedges gleamed wine-coloured and the birches were a mist of palest green. But the nights were bright, with a breath of frost, and all the witchery of unclouded moonshine. In the grey morning silver song from unseen larks, soaring on mist-wet wings; and in the near twilight spoken melody from the mellifluous throats of blackbirds. And the long nights belonged to the owls and the plover which swept, humming and weeping, over cornfield and pasture.

No vixen had yet chosen to whelp in Hackamore, and String Lug, running solitary, denned up there because there were cubs in the scree in Mossrigg. That Keewick should have moved, too, interested him not at all. Using the same tree root which had served him as a cub, he settled in without fuss. He killed only rats at Hackamore Farm, ignoring the hens roosting out, because the place was too near his den. Yet he carried home hens killed elsewhere and left the feathers lying about for all eyes to see. But as few men visited the wood, and Hackamore Farm was not missing hens just then, the litter did not betray him.

One morning he killed a pheasant in a rambling wood called Heatherfield, three miles from home. Feeling crouse after the banquet, he spent a long time playing hide-and-seek with a nimble weasel in a ditch, where it knew every cranny and mousehole. By the time he tired of the game it was long past daylight, so he went back into Heatherfield to lie up for the day. He crossed a lane, trotted gingerly over pebbles at a disused sandpit, pushed through the tall heather from which the wood derived its name, and curled up against a dry peaty bank under a screen of blaeberries.

For half an hour he slept his light fox sleep, with nose to hip and brush covering his eyes. Awakening, he peered through the shimmer of outer hairs and saw a lizard moving towards his face. He flexed a paw to strike, but did not deliver the stroke. At that moment the bark of a terrier came from the direction of the sandpit—a harsh, skirling bark which ripped the air. String Lug was on his feet at the first bark, and away when a crescendo of excited yelping told him that the terrier was running his line.

Jock Simpson, in keeping with his own dictum that a terrier used for going to ground should never be rated for chasing a fox, allowed Corrie to go when he picked up String Lug's scent at the sandpit. At that moment he did not welcome the diversion, for he was on his way to an outlying farm, where foxes with cubs in a deep glen were playing havoc with the poultry. And he was expected at the den in an hour's time, with a dog fit to go to earth. Hoping for once that the dog would soon lose the fox in the heavy cover, or be outrun before he killed himself on his feet, Jock lit his pipe and waited at the sandpit.

The terrier's yelping died away and Jock knew he had reached the common beyond Heatherfield. String Lug, running fast without fear, snaked down a heathery slope through crowded dwarf birches, then crossed a narrow water channel which flowed between waist-high fir plantings to join the burn at the fork. Climbing straight up the opposite rise, he paused at the top, among gorse thick-cushioned by the nibbling of sheep, and watched his back trail. He saw the terrier bellyflap boldly into the water and shake out his coat when he clambered on to the bank. But he did not wait for the yelp of triumph when Corrie picked up the line again. He was halfway across the next field when it came.

String Lug was at the top of the field, on the edge of Sparedrum Wood, when Corrie left the whins. The terrier scampered up the field with tongue flacking, but String Lug ran no farther. He felt confident, now that he had obtained a good view of the dog's dimensions; or perhaps he stopped because he recognized him. Darting into a nettle-choked culvert at the fence, under what had been a road when the Sparedrum pines were seedlings, he faced round tensed for the worry.

Corrie approached the culvert fearlessly, with wire brush birses up, panting but confident. He growled deep in his throat as he thrust through the nettle screen with eyes closed against the stings. Barking harshly, he was in the middle of his snake-quick forward and backward movement, which usually stampeded his quarry or threw it off guard, when the unexpected happened. It was so unusual that he had no immediate or instinctive defence against it.

String Lug struck forward as the terrier danced back, and bit him clean through the lower jaw, getting his own mask pinpricked against the powerful teeth. Corrie howled shrilly and tugged away; and String Lug, who never held, let him go, while preparing for a renewal of the attack. But the terrier was disabled and in pain, and bolted across the fields to his master, yelling his anguish till he found him and whimpering pitifully when Jock examined his jaw.

That wound cost Corrie a month in the hands of a veterinary surgeon, when his life was almost despaired of. The jaw swelled like that of a cow with wooden tongue, and the puncture became septic. When the swelling finally vanished and he recovered, he could no longer deliver lightning-quick strokes on his right side. Jock Simpson combed Heatherfield and Sparedrum for a fox earth, without finding one, and he had no way of knowing that String Lug had come from Hackamore.

Some minutes after Corrie had gone, String Lug emerged warily from the culvert, and pawed at his face, where blood drops were hardening on fur. He was a little nervous, guessing that the dog was not alone and that retribution would be forthcoming. A daylight journey home, risky though it might be, was thus forced on him, and he left at once.

Travelling at a smart fox trot to the whins, already murmurous with bees which crawled unrewarded over nectarless blossoms, he cut left to avoid the wood, and had the cover of the heather till he reached Heatherfield Cottage. In the sandy lane, by the front door, a woman in blue overalls was throwing down grain to hens, while the martins carried mud gathered from the lane-side duck-pond to the cottage eaves. A partridge *krick-ricked* in the field over the hedge. String Lug slipped past without comment from the dog in the barrel kennel and galloped up another lane to the road near Laverock Knowe Farm.

A bright-eyed robin, sitting on a post beside molehills, saw the fox as he squeezed through the hedge, and flitted nervously to a higher sprig of flowering thorn. The robin had been watching the mole at work, ready to fly down when the velvet-coated tunneller turned up creepy crawlers or leatherjackets. A carrion crow barked as String Lug crossed the field, and rooks with full pouches came from nowhere to mob him till he reached the glen.

From a whin outcrop, lichened and moss-bearded, and yellow spotted with tormentil, he saw a man with two greyhounds far down the road. And presently he smelled cat and dog below a birch in a rock-clustered washout. In the first fork of the tree a yellow tom-cat clung precariously, whimpering as he pawed at his broken face, and too preoccupied with the greyhound's trade mark to notice the fox below him.

String Lug reached Hackamore as the cows were turned out to pasture, brown and white, black and white, dappled and red, and sleek and clean as good husbandry could make them. He lay in the shade of trees near the pasture fence, lick-licking at his coat, while a cuckoo at the wood end called monotonously. For half an hour he lay day-dreaming, listening to the hum and buzz of flies, to the lowing of cattle and the far voices of men in the fields. Birdsong trickled like raindrops through the trees. Rising lazily at last, he stretched himself, yawned, chewed grass and went to bed.

That night he killed a duck at Mossrigg, which was not missed by Gallacher for two days, and then presumed lost with no mention of foxes. String Lug did not spoil the delusion by going back for more—too soon. For a week he moved little beyond Hackamore, finding excellent hunting at the west corner, where swarms of young rabbits suddenly appeared in the pasture. He thinned them out quickly, and fed to repletion, but soon hankered for a change of diet. His thoughts ran to feathered prey, with the emphasis on pheasant. So, one windless night, when the moon's first crescent was a silver cat's claw unsheathed from a purple paw of cloud, he went out to explore the double hedge bordering the Hackamore hayfield, which that season reached right down to the fringe of Brockhurst.

Crossing the big cornfield to the hedge, he picked up a loud-voiced escort of agitated peewits, whose flight marked his line through the corn. They swooped *weep-weeping*, rolling and banking above his head on rounded wings which hummed as the wind sang in the webs of feathers. They curled close as he trotted with studied nonchalance, almost brushing his face with wing-tips, and trailing feet over the corn blades when they cuvred steeply to renew the assault from behind.

The assault of wings, and the vibrant, far-carrying cries, forced String Lug into hiding till they should forget him. In the hedge bottom he lay down, still and invisible, crushing charlock and folded crowns of hogweed, and screened by the thick, feather-topped grasses. Soon the keening music ceased, and the birds returned to eggs or stilt-legged chicks squatting moveless in the corn.

String Lug nosed scents between the hedges, a darker shadow in the darkened lane, treading noiselessly and belly-tickled by the grass tops. In the tangle grew stray stalks of oats and wheat, from seeds which had trickled from holed sacks at sowing time. Coming suddenly on a hedgehog beside a brier, he pulled up short, with head drawn back, and reached out at it with a paw. The hedgehog, with brow quills forward, crouched like a carving till the paw tipped him under the snout, when he tucked in his head and hoped for the best. String Lug, having little experience of hedgehogs, sat down to ponder the armoured ball. He had a notion to try to solve the riddle on the spot, until his nose thrilled to the merest trace of pheasant smell from under the brier.

A hen pheasant sat on eleven near-hatching eggs, below a lean-to of tall grass in the heart of the brier. She had seen the hedgehog and was little worried; but she couldn't see the fox, though she guessed his presence.

HE TROTTED WITH STUDIED NONCHALANCE

String Lug crashed into the brier without warning, prepared to snatch. The impetus of his spring was slowed by the resilience of the brier stems, which gave the pheasant a split second to make arrangements to save her life. She burst out of the brier in a frenzy of wings, leaving breast feathers and rump plumes hooked on thorns. String Lug landed with one foot in the nest and a thorn in the pad of the other. He pulled the thorn with his teeth, then ate all the unborn chicks with their unabsorbed yolk sacs attached. Licking his lips, he returned to the hedgehog, which had not moved during the turmoil.

The hedgehog's peace of mind—perhaps its life—was saved, unintentionally, by a weasel. Away across the cornfield, where the lane-side trees shut out the moon, a rabbit screamed. It was a cry of anguish and despair, thin but piercing, which sent up String Lug's ear. Looking longingly at the hedgehog, he rolled it over with a paw and submitted it to the outrage of defilement. He itched to stay; but, knowing what the rabbit's scream meant, he raced towards the sound.

He found the rabbit with little difficulty. The weasel's trade mark was on it, for its neck was warm and sticky with blood; but String Lug saw no sign of the killer, though he could smell its musk. As he trotted away with the rabbit he heard the weasel chipping, with its triangular head sticking out of a molehill. But he was in no mood to waste time and energy chasing a will-o'-the-wisp with such a specialized knowledge of subterranean geography.

Nightly, for the next week or so, he visited the double hedge, without finding any more late-nesting pheasants. He caught mice, many mice, and destroyed a family of six in a hayball nest in a tussock. One night, when the moon was past the full and Keewick was hunting bats above the hayfield, he met a fox cub in the lane. The cub was a precocious youngster with most of his milk teeth,

a tousie coat and a cloistered outlook on life. In his jaws
he was carrying an old condensed milk tin which had
been his favourite toy, and which he had taken with
him when, for reasons known only to himself, he had left
home before his time to face the world alone.

String Lug was poking in the hedge bottom for mouse
nests when the cub sauntered up with all the easy confidence of the very young. He carried his little brush gay
and his tin by the saw-edged lid. He heard Keewick *wick-
wicking* and cocked his ears. Then he heard the swish of
grass, and tried to look round. With his mouth full, he
could do nothing to protect himself when a big fox, twice
his height and thrice his weight, launched at him from the
hedge shadow. Before he fully realized what was happening he had his face ripped from eye to whiskers. He
jumped when String Lug snatched at his pads, dropped
his tin, and streaked for the hayfield with a snarling
demon at his heels.

Birds rose in startled flight when String Lug raced
through the ripe hay—two partridges, a hen pheasant
and many twittering moss-cheepers. Away to the right a
roe deer bounded from the hay, having first tossed the
twin fawns she had been nursing into new lies among
the timothy and cocksfoot. They crouched motionless,
with velvet muzzles against dappled flanks, with no moon
highlight in their eyes and little body scent—the most
exquisitely beautiful of all the children of the wild.

String Lug gave up the chase at the Brockhurst dyke,
having twice nipped the fleeing cub in the rump, and
turned back into the hay. He had not attacked the cub
just because he was spiteful and it was small. He did so
because he was a fox, and would have acted in the same
way had it been the cub's father or the biggest dog fox
ever whelped.

On his way back he missed the fawns and thirteen
downy partridge chicks, but noted the much-used runs

of hare and rabbit. At the hedge he stopped and shook his head vigorously to get rid of the hayseed. In the silence after his shaking he heard the brush of wings on stone, and rushed to the spot. Suddenly his nose filled with the smell of rook, and in the same moment he saw the bird dragging away.

The rook had been disabled—with a broken wing— since the flapper shooting in the rookery near Summerfield Farm weeks before, and had walked to the hayfield after many nerve-racking chases by cats, dogs and children. There he had found sanctuary, feeding on leatherjackets, wireworms and the eggs of small birds. The rook rolled on his side as the fox caught up with him, and tried to fight with beak, feet and uninjured wing. But String Lug's teeth clicked once and the bird was dead. For a minute afterwards it flapped its wings and bit its tongue with the tips of its mandibles, while the fox pinned it down with a paw. Then it lay still, a warm rag of feathers in the hay.

Picking up the body, which was light and skinny, String Lug carried it away with him. All the cows in the Hackamore pasture rose from their cud-chewing and followed him with lowered heads right to the woodside fence. When he slipped through they shambled away to press out new beds in the damp grass and chew stolidly till the birds sang at daybreak. String Lug deposited his rook on a mossed stump, lay down and started to tongue the hayseed from his coat. But he soon gave it up and attacked his toes instead, for the webs were tickly and irritated by the pull-through of seeding grass and clover. When he went to bed his feet still itched. . . .

In the morning a low mist like frost smoke lay over the pasture and circled the trees with moveless ringlets. It hid the cows which were lying down and revealed only the backs of those which grazed. String Lug stayed abed till the mist lifted in the sun's warmth, and swallows hunting low for flies above dung pats returned to barns and stables with undamped wings. Then he came out to doze in a sun patch.

Later he lay just inside the fence, screened by grass and red campion and with the dead rook beside him, watching a cow chewing the cud while she wagged her great ears to chase the flies. The ripples on her neck when food passed up her gullet intrigued him, till the flies found his own ears and eyes and he was forced to go under cover again. This time he took the dead rook with him and curled up with it against his cheek.

Before he went hunting that night he played with the dead rook, then placed it with much care in his burrow. It was still too fresh to interest him overmuch, but he had no intention of losing it through carelessness. When he left the wood the night was close and breathless with no moon and no leaf trembling. Travelling south through pastures and cornfields and three strips of wood, he reached a slope, pockmarked with holes and hillocky with shale, where coal outcrops had been worked many years before. It was a region much frequented by rabbits, cadaverous in the fattest summer and fluke-ridden in wet winters. But no rabbit was out among the ragwort on the slope, a fox having passed that way earlier. The taint he left behind him kept the rabbits below ground. String Lug was taking a last sniff at the fox scent when the storm broke, and he had to rush into a gummy cavern for shelter.

Through the short, wind-shaken night he stayed in his shelter, while the trees were lashed and battered and the ditches ran full. Lightning flashed near and far, throwing into relief the tossing tops of trees, black against a livid sky. String Lug was not afraid of the lightning, but he cowered in fear when the thunder crashed and rumbled in the tormented dark.

At first daylight the wind died and the rain pattered

to a smir, the purr of which could not be heard above the swish and gurgle of water in a hundred new channels worn on the slope in the night. Owls hunted belatedly when the sun's red rim gilded the eastern sky, and birds flapped wet wings or clawed fiercely at rain-itching ears. String Lug stalked stiffly from his refuge with dirtied fur and an empty belly.

From the farm at the top of the slope hens scrambled out to forage, while ducks quacked as they laid eggs on the strawy floor of the closed duckhouse. String Lug sneaked to the scrawny hedge, down the other side of which the hens were flapping and squawking on their way to the cornfield below. The flighty ones launched into the air from the breast of the slope and flew the rest of the way, with much clapping of wings and hysterical screeching.

Instead of waiting till the birds reached the cover of the corn, String Lug rushed impetuously through the hedge when they were in the middle of their wild scamper. If his attack was rash, his timing was flawless. A white hen with a scarlet comb rose as he snatched, but he caught her before she was two feet in the air and killed her while she cackled her alarm. A woman appeared at the door of the farmhouse as String Lug raced back through the hedge, and he knew he had been seen. So he did not linger; nor did he bolt for home across the open fields. Instead, he followed a deep gully, with rowans and birches growing close among bracken on the slopes, and choked at the bottom with meadowsweet and woundwort, angelica and avens, and shuddering grass tall enough to hide a cow.

He came into Hackamore from the north, through the pasture. The cows stood at gaze till he slipped into the wood and Pica, the magpie, flew chattering down the field, where a sick herring gull stood moping with dropped wings. A miner, cycling to his work, spied the fox entering the wood, and passed the news to the McLeod brothers when he reached the farm. In the course of the day Colin McLeod learned that Knowehead Farm had lost a hen and seen the fox; and Knowehead learned where the fox was lying.

Six men crossed the pasture in the late afternoon, confident, fed, and armed with shotguns. There were Gallacher of Mossrigg, the McLeod brothers and three men from Knowehead. String Lug, engrossed in observing the phenomenon of regurgitation in cows, saw them when they entered the field and guessed at once that they were calling on him. He was out of the wood and two miles away before they found the remains of his breakfast and Gallacher recognized the feathers of his own Khaki Campbell duck. Feeling more confident than ever about rising a fox, they carried on stolidly to the wood end, where they were hailed suddenly by a loud voice with a laugh in it.

"It's foxhounds ye'll need noo. Your fox broke oot before I left the glen and should be nearly at Wallace's Monument by this time!" It was Jock Simpson, arriving late and unarmed for the drive.

"Must ha'e seen us," said Gallacher to the others. Then to Jock: "Hoo's the dug?"

"Mendin', Wull, mendin', but a wee pookit yet. We micht as well try Mossrigg noo that the artillery's oot. There's foxes there gettin' too much peace."

And to Mossrigg they went, while String Lug sat in the whins beyond Heatherfield studying the ways of ants.

# Chapter Ten

## HARVEST

S'TRING LUG RETURNED TO HACKAMORE THE FOLLOWING morning, before sunrise, coming in against a southwest wind which rushed through the trees and rolled unattended cushat eggs from wafer nests in high, whippy branches. Pica, seeing the fox in the gloaming, *chuck-ucked* in anger. Rabbits sat up momentarily in praying attitude, with ears pointing skywards, before moving into the wood in a body. String Lug caught only stray whiffs of their funk smell, for all scent was wind-scattered that morning. But he knew when he nosed their runs that they had gone only after the magpie's warning.

Before he went into the wood he made a cast the entire length of the fence with his nose seeking man scent. Though not unduly worried by the visit of the men, he was testing every yard of the way in case they had left reminders. String Lug had acquired much wisdom, without repeat lessons, and not the least of that wisdom was his preparedness to meet what he least expected. So he looked out for men when men were abed just as carefully as he did when they were out of it. And he remained trapwary long after Pate Tamson had given up trapping in disgust. But he learned another lesson about haying time which no previous experience had equipped him to guard against.

During a spell of wet, windy weather he killed three hens at Mossrigg and two at Summerfield, visiting Gallacher and Cameron on alternate nights and taking only one bird each time. He carried out his raids on the farms with as much caution and suspicion as a fox on a first visit and expecting interruption. Tempers became frayed and Gallacher tried in vain to induce tree-roosting hens to use houses under lock and key. Then Summerfield lost a third hen, killed early, but in daylight. Cameron, rushing into the stackyard when he heard the cackling of hens, waved and shouted, and got close enough to String Lug to recognize his torn ear. But all his shouting and gesticulating did not make him drop his hen.

Cameron rushed to the fence to see which way the fox would run, and watched him follow the hedge to the wood. String Lug did not stop running till he reached the rookery, in the farthest neck of the wood beyond the burn. Dropping the hen among thick raspberry canes, he lay down beside it to listen. It was an hour before he started to pluck it. When he had eaten the entrails and part of the breast, he covered the rest of it with leaves and sought a tree root to doze under till nightfall. Rooks, still feeding young in the branches, cawed their alarm when they spied him below, and protested loudly till hungry fledglings needed feeding again.

At first darkening String Lug went home by dyke and hedgerow, after eating the remainder of his prey in the rookery. He crossed the burn opposite Hackamore Farm and went straight up the slope without shaking his wet feet. Keewick, hunting mice among the bushes, swerved and *wick-wicked* loudly when he saw the fox leaving the whins.

String Lug slept till late in the afternoon, then spent the rest of the daylight nosing through the wood in search of mice and birds' nests. In the half-darkness of a cloudless midnight he cut across the open fields and trotted down the wheel-rutted lane to Summerfield Farm. He knew where hens roosted on bales of straw in an open barn; and he knew how to approach the barn.

With a paw on the first bale he halted, uneasy and suspicious. With both forepaws on the bale, he sniffed at the hens in the darkest corner of the barn, and felt uneasier than ever. So he jumped down lightly and drew away. In the dark a shotgun spat flame and pellets, and started the hens gossiping. The shot ploughed the litter near String Lug, sending a cloud of husks and dust into his face. A window opened when he bolted. He heard its screak, but he did not hear the language of Cameron who had sat up with loaded gun because he had a notion that it was his turn again.

The incident ruffled String Lug without blunting his appetite for poultry. When he reached the top of the lane he halted, pawed eyes and nose savagely, and scratched his ears. Thinking over his next move, he dawdled down the road. Arriving at the Hackamore Farm close, he had a notion to go in when a car suddenly switched on headlights and started towards him with much grinding of gears. The late traveller saw twin orbs of green without wondering what they were, and Colin McLeod was too busy saying "Good night" to see String Lug darting out of the beam.

Not till McLeod's step in the yard was followed by the slamming of a door did String Lug sneak past the close and continue his road journey. At the bend beyond the farm fresh whin chips had been scattered on poured tar, but he picked his way distastefully over them without quitting the road. Between the high trees of Summerfield and Brockhurst the road was wet and the air cold. The mossy dykes sweated moisture. String Lug soon reached the bridge at the burn, and turned right for Mossrigg Farm.

At the farm road end he felt for the wind and drew into the yard, through a jungle of grass, ragwort, hogweed and great moon daisies. On the stackyard edge he stood for one minute, belly deep in sneezewort and hemp nettle, and with grass seed sticking to his nose.

But there were no free hens in Mossrigg that night, Gallacher's wife having got them indoors by the simple expedient of calling them up for grain, throwing it inside the laying houses and shutting doors and popholes when they went in to feed. String Lug examined every house and hankered without result; but he detected hen smell under a thorn tree near the gable end of the byre. He found the source of the smell easily enough and stopped to ponder the phenomenon with head askew.

On a flat board lay the chopped-up liver and entrails of a hen, with the head and a few feathers added as trimmings. The mixture had been prepared by Gallacher, doctored with rat poison—the best, or worst, he had—and laid out when the collies were safely kennelled and the cats indoors. String Lug had no suspicion of the mixture, but was annoyed because it could not be carried away. It had to be eaten on the spot. He did eat part of it, mostly liver, then stopped abruptly, with his tongue clicking against the roof of his mouth. The taste was not displeasing, but it was not right. And the more he clicked his tongue the more he became certain that it was very far from being right. Suddenly suspicious, he stepped back, hesitated, nosed his flank, turned and—bolted. . . .

In Hackamore he rummaged among the ferns in a hollow, chewing, clicking his teeth, and gurrying savagely. He vomited twice before he sought his den—bright-eyed, leg-weary, and with griping pains in his belly. Unsleeping, he came out to vomit a third time, coughing, retching, and shaking his slimy tongue, while his belly gulped and his eyes ran water. For two days he was a very sick fox, sleeping most of the time, drinking little and eating not at all. At half-past two on the morning of the third day he came out, famished, thinner, a little queasy in the stomach, but as fit and alert as he had been before he tasted Gallacher's mixture. His legs were his own again, and he was hungry for everything except poultry.

Between the hedges at the hayfield he stalked and caught a fat partridge brooding five chicks in the grass.

The cock, covering six chicks in the hedge bottom, escaped with his share of the brood, but three of the five with the mother died. String Lug ate all three chicks on the spot, fluff and all, and carried the hen to the hayfield. The cock partridge called up the two remaining cheepers, and puffed himself up bigger to cover them. At break of day he led them into the safety of the cornfield.

String Lug had to cross ten yards of swathe to reach the standing hay, for cutting had begun while he was ill abed. The air was fragrant with the sweetness of it, and its touch was cool on the pads. In a few minutes he had trodden out a bed in the thick hay, and started to pluck his partridge. He had bitten the bird through the neck, and the fresh blood put new life in him when he licked it in. He ate it all except the beak, feet and feathers, made a hasty toilet, and curled up, prepared to spend the rest of the night in the hay and hunt his breakfast there at the dawning.

But he overslept because this was his first real resting sleep for three days, and because he had no idea how old the darkness was when he left his lair. The sun was high in the sky of clear blue when he woke up, and the hay-scented air was noisy as a sawmill with clouds of flies. Clegs bored in vain for a way through his thick fur, while he pawed them from his face and chopped them into blood splashes on his legs. Rising, he shook out hayseed and yawned. He examined the wind's breath, picking out the scent of birds and roe, despite the heavy odour of the hay.

Fifty yards away, in a hoof-trodden lie, twin roe fawns stood face-licking and milk happy. Though able to follow the doe, she was content to leave them in the safety of the hay a little longer. String Lug soon pointed the fawns, thrilling to the smell of them. With the wind dead on his nose he started to walk up to them, scarcely disturbing the hay in his passage. Before he reached them he heard the distant voices of men and the bluttering of a tractor. Without an instant's hesitation, he forgot roe and turned back to the edge of the cut to see what was afoot.

The tractor came into the hayfield with Colin McLeod in the driving seat and two youths hanging on behind. String Lug watched with much interest and no fear while McLeod, in shirt-sleeves, fixed up the reaper and directed the youths to the root field, where they were going to hoe swedes. Nor did he go when the tractor began its noisy, untiring, monotonous run. He moved farther into the cover and lay down panting sweat, while the hay wavered and fell in shimmering swathes, and the smell of exhaust smoke and hot oil tormented his nostrils.

String Lug had no fear of one man and a tractor, and he knew exactly just what was taking place. Yet he was cautious enough to avoid moving about after birds or roe in case he betrayed his presence. At the moment he was content to stay. In his own time he would leave discreetly.

Late in the forenoon, when the sun shone with blast furnace heat and the clegs were desperate, the tractor stopped, and he heard once more the voices of men. Peering through the screen he saw two men and a woman approaching McLeod. One of the men was Sandy from Hackamore, red-faced, red-headed, wearing spectacles, and up to take over the cutting after the morning break. The other two were from the village and carried guns for the rabbits which they knew would almost certainly be lying up in the last of the hay. Presently the turnip men arrived for bread and cheese. And String Lug knew it was time for him to go.

When he climbed the dyke into Brockhurst he was amazed to see another fox running into the hay from the direction of the cattle trough. Guessing that the fox had been risen in the wood, he watched carefully without showing himself, and before long saw a man with a black dog coming out of the hollow, headed for the party seated round the tractor.

Jock Simpson spoke to McLeod while the black bitch fussed round the mistress of Hackamore, pawing her shoulder till she was given a bread-and-cheese sandwich from the basket.

"Nae deer yet, Jock," said Colin. "But they micht lie up a wee longer. There's a pickle hay standin' yet."

"There's a kid there sure," was the reply. "I saw it go in wi' the auld doe late last nicht. I'll send the bitch in, onyway, an' make sure." Colin had cut the legs off a fawn with the reaper the previous year and wanted to avoid a similar experience again if he could. "Wan run through should dae," Jock went on, "an' if the artillery boys take a side apiece in front o' her they should get ony rabbits that bolt."

"Here's Pate wi' his dug," Sandy interrupted, pointing.

"Best tell him to keep it up in case there *is* a deer," said Jock. "That beast could run doon a kid an' brek its back afore ye could say *don't*."

"Deers," said the moocher when McLeod told him to hold the dog. "Long says deers wastes trees."

"We're fermers, Pate; no' foresters," replied Colin very quietly. And Pate looped a string in the lurcher's collar.

When String Lug saw the men with guns coming round the top side of the hay he hurried quietly down the inside of the dyke to a spot opposite the bottom end of the cut. There, hidden by knapweed and ragwort, he lay down to watch. His curiosity was consuming him, and he still had absolute confidence in his ability to deal with any emergency which might arise. He watched the guns move into position, with Jock Simpson in the centre of the cut. Sandy and the turnip-thinners stood back while the mistress packed cups with hay and Pate held the lurcher close to the tractor. A cushat flew into the tree above

String Lug's head, and crooned, and he knew that those sharpest of eyes had failed to detect him.

Jock waved the bitch into the hay, and the men followed her progress by watching the swaying tops. She was hardly in her stride when she put out a gaudy cock pheasant—tailless and terrified.

Sandy guffawed: "It's nae tail. The dug must've bited it aff!"

The first two rabbits out were rolled over and picked up, but the third was missed and scuttered for the wood. A very young leveret, with long whiskers, and wavy fur flecked with silver, was allowed to go unmolested. The bitch moved forward steadily, with nose to the ground, snoaking incessantly while her otter tail wagged above the hay tops. Presently two partridges rose from the edge of the left-hand cut, one to whir away like a cannon ball on down-pointed wings, the other to flutter in mock disablement along the ground. They had gone into the hay just before the arrival of McLeod with the tractor. One of the turnip-thinners ran to pick up the bird, shouting: "The dug must ha'e but it!" Both he and Sandy had the same trouble with the verb "to bite".

"But your granmaw," yelled Sandy in derision. "It's only shammin'. Isn't it, hen?" he said to the dog when she came out with cocked ears to look after the bird.

Jock spoke to the dog and halted the guns. "Fetch them oot, lass!" he said to her. "Gently!"

In she went again while the men stood round. String Lug, reaching up to see what was happening, snarled when the cushat left its perch with a clatter of white-barred wings. He had forgotten about the bird. But no one paid any attention to it as it swung out over the hay on whistling wings. String Lug saw the bitch make nine journeys from the hay to her master, but he could not see the nine partridge chicks which she delivered to his hands. Nor could he understand what Jock was doing when he put them down gently in the double hedge, where the old bird soon called them up.

String Lug wondered about the fox when he saw the dog return to the hay, and was surprised when he saw her bolt out again almost immediately. She had her ears pinned back and her tail between her legs.

"She must have seen a moose!" said one of the guns.

Jock Simpson laughed. Sandy rubbed his chin and said: "If ye get they guns ready ye'll likely fin that the moose has black-tipped lugs, a bushy tail an' a taste for jucks an' pooltry. I've saw that bitch meet a fox afore!"

String Lug saw Jock step back out of the way with the dog while Sandy and the youths raked about in the hay. The fox came out with a dash, a dog fox with a good brush and the right kind of swerve to upset poking shots. Both guns roared twice, but the fox carried on, unhurt, without looking back.

"Thanks for cuttin' some swathes o' hay," said Sandy sarcastically. "The beast wagged its tail at ye!"

Sandy was cut short when McLeod roared suddenly: "Pate! Send Sam!"

The lurcher was loosened as he spoke, for Pate had been ready for just such an opportunity. The dog galloped across the field at a tremendous pace. A cross between a greyhound and a Bedlington terrier, he was bigger than any greyhound, with a wiry coat, a long jaw, and a nose like a foxhound. The fox raced for the wood, but turned when a car stopped and the occupants jumped out to watch the chase. As he ran up the inside of the dyke at the field end, the lurcher cut the angle, shot forward in a lightning spurt, and reached for him as he gained the hedge. The fox twisted round, fighting gamely; but Sam broke his neck before Pate arrived with a hammer from the tractor tool-box. While the men clustered round Pate, congratulating the lurcher, a roe fawn broke from the hay and bounded in terror to the road.

"There it goes noo," said Jock to McLeod, "near oot o' itsel wi' fricht!"

Sandy swung up to the driving seat of the tractor and the youths walked away to the root-field. The moocher left with the fox over his shoulder and Sam mouthing it from behind. The guns left with the mistress of Hackamore, who was allowed to carry her own basket. Sandy made two rounds with the tractor while Jock and McLeod stood talking, and while String Lug, still in the same place, sat watching a brown butterfly, with bull's-eyes on its wings, fluttering from knapweed to knapweed. When Sandy started his third round the men left and walked slowly towards the gate in the double hedge.

In the act of closing the gate behind them they looked back suddenly when Sandy yelled to them to come back. The moocher, who had loitered to wait for them, turned back too. Sandy was running his fingers through his red hair when they reached the tractor.

"There was twa o' them," he said regretfully, pointing to a roe fawn which he had cut to pieces with the reaper. "I'm awfu' vexed." Colin looked at him curiously, surprised at his apologetic tone, for he had always considered Sandy a man without feelings.

String Lug saw Jock and Pate carrying something to the wood and dropping it inside the dyke. He rose as they walked back to the tractor and, for reasons known only to himself, chose the moment that Jock looked round to jump on to the dyke, with his four feet bunched together and his brush hanging slack. Jock caught Pate by the arm and pointed, and String Lug jumped into the open field as the lurcher was waved out in his direction. He took the same route as the first fox, and Sam swung left to head him. But String Lug suddenly turned sharp right, shot over the dyke, crossed the road, and streaked flat out through a field of corn.

With a lead of a hundred yards, he swung right at the

first fence and gained the cover of Summerfield before the lurcher could cut his line on the angle. He rose a hare as he blundered into massed rhododendrons. He circled two trees, and was running through the heavy growth on the wood edge when Sam climbed the dyke from the field. String Lug was determined to slow the dog to the speed of its nose. On the low ground beside the burn he thrust through meadowsweet and foxglove, through massed spikes of stinking woundwort, and great thickets of angelica and withering wild liquorice. Splashing across the burn, he shook out his fur and raced into a small meadow of scraggy hay near a road. Unwinded, he was content to wait and see what was going to happen. And he knew a hole across the road to which he could run if need be.

Presently Sam climbed out of the burn and ran the fox's line true to the meadow. Sam was patient and wise, and came on without noise. He crossed the meadow, following by scent alone, and heard the roar of a motor cycle on the road. String Lug, unworried by the dog, but annoyed by the inopportune arrival of the motor cycle, rushed to the gate with Sam twenty yards behind. He crossed as the motor cycle rounded the bend, and was through the hedge on the other side when Sam reached the gate. The lurcher shot on to the road just as the startled cyclist reached the gate. String Lug heard the screech of tyres, the howling of a dog, and a crash—then silence. He waited for a moment to see if Sam would come through the hedge: but no Sam appeared. String Lug, uncertain about what had happened, went to ground to think the matter over.

Sam and the motor cyclist were both taken to Summerfield Farm in a van which came along soon after String Lug disappeared underground. The cyclist was bruised and stunned, and Sam had a damaged shoulder.

When String Lug left his refuge at dusk the motor

cycle had been removed and he had no way of knowing what had taken place. Having a good memory, and an insatiable curiosity, he hurried straight to Brockhurst to discover what the men had left down in the wood. He soon found the mutilated roe fawn and grinned his appreciation of his own cleverness. And in the leaf-scented dusk, while Keewick hooted and the swifts hunted high, he tasted venison for the first time in his life.

# Chapter Eleven

## GOLDEN DAYS

S<small>UMMER DIED WHEN THE CUCKOOS FLED AND THE</small> curlews left the moor. Swallows hunted feverishly from misty sunrise to crimson sunset for third broods hatched in barns and stables, and cushats fed squeakers with corn from stook and stubble. Ash and sycamore gave first leaves to the wind, while the hedgerows were still bright with the yellow of ragwort, vetchling and trefoil, the wine red of clover, thistle and knapweed, the blurred purple of tufted vetch and the china-delicate blue of harebell.

In cloudless, sunny weather the corn was cut, and cushats from Brockhurst, Summerfield, Hackamore and Scandinavia fed on the stooks or settled in the waving, yellow wheat. When the fieldfares came the elder berries were purpling and acorns needed only strong winds to loosen them. The partridge coveys picked stubble corn, leaving the leatherjackets to the rooks, who paid for their grain by eating them. By night weasels hunted mice in the stubbles with Keewick and Tufter, while the air grew cold and roe bucks fed alone.

These were fat days for String Lug, when he played the corn-stook trick on cushats and partridges, and ambushed hens turned on to the stubbles in the morning. They were golden days of glistering sun and crimsoning haws; blue days when plover wheeled in keening flight against a sky like a shilfa's head; short days of noise and warm harvest scents, when men sweated and red-nostrilled, heaving horses pulled heavy farm wagons into stackyards littered with grain and dusty straw. Hedge-hogs grew fat for the long sleep; and mice stored grain and berries against the lean days of the hunger moon.

String Lug was sleeping soundly in a sun-warmed ditch on a breezy afternoon, after the first of the wheat had been cut and a few hours before the world went to war. War was an affair of men—those animals with souls and intellects—so his dream was not disturbed. He woke with his world unchanged, normal hunger in his belly, and no knowledge whatever of death or to-morrow. But his world had changed, though he did not know it, as all too soon he would learn.

Jock Simpson and Robert, the schoolmaster's son, walked through the stooks of the Hackamore wheatfield in the yellow brilliance of that same evening, while rooks blackened the stubbles and gulls sailed on wide wings in the glare of the low sun. As they approached the dyke at Summerfield a partridge covey exploded into the air from the crowded molehills where they had been scratching.

"The first cannon balls o' the war," said Jock with a gravity completely alien to him. As he spoke Robert gripped his arm. One of the mole heaps had moved. It not only moved: it rose and ran away down the dykeside, on four blue-black legs, with brush flying.

"The same wan again," said Jock, without addressing Robert. "That beast'll no dee bose." Then to Robert: "That's the fox that near broke Gallacher's heart, the wan he tried tae pizen. . . ."

"But how can you tell?" Robert was perplexed. "They all look alike to me!"

"Man, ye get tae ken differences when ye look long enough. An' that beast has only wan lug that works. I've been close to him often when he disna ken. I widna wunner it was him led Pate's dug the dance. An' he'll hae nothing tae dae wi' doctored hens laid oot for him. He cocks a snoot and lets them be!"

"Do you think . . .?" Robert began. "I mean, is it

HE PLAYED THE CORN-STOOK TRICK

possible he hoped those birds would mistake him for a molehill and come close enough for him to catch one?"

Jock laughed. "Like enough! An' they micht hae got plenty o' fleas at that—if they'd leeved long enough tae get started scratchin'!"

String Lug did not run far when he saw that the men were unarmed and without dogs. When he reached the burn he stopped, and flung himself down heavily below a goat willow which dipped its outermost leaves in the sun-dappled current. Hot after playing at molehills, he lay with tongue shuddering and dripping sweat. He rose when a beady-eyed vole scurried over a pebbly ridge, just below the trailing willow tips, and caught it in the act of diving into deeper water. The vole, which squeaked at the grip of his teeth, was sleek and fat, and made him forget his huff at being baulked of partridges.

At moonrise, when roosting magpies chattered in suspicion of shadow movement which was nothing more alarming than tree branches stirred by the wind, he trotted through the stooks of the Hackamore wheatfield, travelling round two sides of the uncut square and keeping the wind in his face. The dry stalks pricked his pads, but there was no crickle of splintering straw at his footfalls. On the second corner of the cut he froze and sorted out scents with his wet nose. Damp, autumn smell of earth and stubble, sweet smell of ripe wheat, trace taint of weasel musk, ghost of warm cow smell from the farm two hundred yards away. . . . Then he had it—scent of partridges, faint, some distance upwind, and difficult to plot. But he could own it. With head up and nostrils aquiver, he noted the layout—wind direction, distance, position of stooks and shadows—and with every move figured went in to the stalk.

The partridge covey was sleeping in the shadow of a stook, facing the wind and side on to the moon. String Lug edged a little to the right, till he had a line of stooks

ahead leading right up to the covey. With the moon in his
face, he dodged from stook to stook, crossing each moonlit space boldly because he knew he would not be exposed
to the view of the birds. Suddenly he stopped, when his
nose received wind warning of approaching men. Slipping
under the cover of a stook, he tested the air for dog smell,
but found none. So he sat still to wait for the men.

Two men with a long net for rabbits came down the
field, walking slowly with swish and crackle of boots on
brittle stubble. String Lug heard a *krick-rick* of query
from the partridges, and quivered when the men loomed
close in the moonlight. The men stopped, startled, when
the partridges burst almost from their feet, *airking* like
corncrakes as they whirred away across the field.

String Lug watched the men into Summerfield, and
came out of hiding as Keewick crossed the moon's face
on downy wings, with a young weasel snatched from a
stook in his claws. Pigeons flew in the moonlight when the
poachers were in the wood. In the heavy shadows of the
elms near the boundary fence above the burn, a partridge
was fluttering along the ground. It scrambled away,
terrified but silent, when it saw the fox. For a moment
String Lug stood watching, having been fooled before by
the distraction display of a mother partridge. But the
bird had blood scent on it, and he realized that it was
ground flapping because it could do no other. That afternoon the bird had been wounded by the man who had the
shooting of Hackamore Farm, a city man who owned no
retriever, and whose only regret about runners was that he
missed them in the bag.

With the partridge flapping in his jaws, String Lug
crawled under a stook, tore off most of the feathers, and
ate it with much lip-licking, holding it between his forepaws while he chewed with the side of his mouth. He
hankered to stay in the stook afterwards, but sneezed
fluff and went home instead, knowing that men would be

working in the field in the morning. Keewick, sitting puff-feathered, with craw bulging and half a weasel held under his claws, bubbled as the fox squeezed under the fence. Nearby three young owls turned heads to stare silently down. Neither Keewick nor his mate ever drove away their grown family, being content to wait till they left of their own accord.

The yattering of magpies and the leathery slap of cushat wings in the morning sent up String Lug's ear in sleep, and the message flashed to his brain. He peered through the screening roots as a hare ducked under the fence with flattened ears. Lassie, the collie from Hackamore Farm, sailed between wires close behind, yelping because she knew she was losing the race. Keewick wafted from his perch when the bitch flashed under his tree and String Lug drew into the depths of his burrow. Presently the bitch came back, winded and gulping air. She stopped when she got the smell of fox and rushed in a wolf crouch to the bottom of the tree. She sniffed and growled while her hackles rose, then started to dig furiously under the root, yelping her excitement and biting at the fibre in the soil.

Damp earth showered through the root tendrils, while String Lug thought quickly and Keewick watched curiously from a distance. When the bitch had dug down her own length, and was becoming frantic at the strong fox smell, String Lug squeezed out of his back door and slipped unobtrusively away. Lassie scraped on for some minutes before she realized that the musk smell was becoming less strong. In a frenzy lest she was being fooled, she pulled out and sniffed every nearby hole, just as she did when she was digging for rabbits. But she did not smell at String Lug's back door, though she crossed his escape line without appearing to notice it.

Just then Bounce, solitary since the rut, stepped daintily from the trees. Lassie, shaking soilings from her coat, immediately gave chase. Bounce sailed effortlessly over the fence and bounded gracefully down the pasture, with Lassie chasing and losing pace by barking. McLeod, at the burn, seeing the bitch, called her in with a shrill whistle. Before she reached him, with tail down, String Lug was hedge-trotting in the Knowehead cornfield, thinking hard over the collie's visit.

A return to his den was out of the question meantime. Lassie would come again, and sooner or later McLeod would come with her; and the back door through which he had escaped from the collie could prove a death-trap if McLeod happened along at the wrong moment with a couple of terriers. And String Lug did not relish the idea of having one terrier at his face, another at his back, with a collie sitting on the doorstep and men with guns perhaps standing by. With a solid wall at his back, he feared no terrier, but he couldn't fight back and front at once.

For nearly a week he slept out, usually among bracken When he did settle in again it was in the hole under the scaur in Laverock Knowe wood, which had been used by his mate in the spring. Rabbits had worked at the hole since it was deserted, sending galleries left and right under the whin. The ground held the print of many feet, and dry pellets of dung lay thick outside. No rabbits were at home when he went in; nor did any return after he had taken over.

Though there were many pheasants in Laverock Knowe, none of them roosted on the ground, so String Lug had to hunt them in daylight when they were foraging in stubble, roots or potatoes, or under oaks and beeches. He was most successful in the potatoes, where he could lie hidden in the drills and chop the heads off unwary birds poking under the shaws as they fed.

One day the Mossrigg Farm shooting tenant drove a field of potatoes without dogs, blattering at every pheasant or partridge whether the distance was eight yards or eighty. String Lug bolted and nearly collided with a woman in check tweeds, who waited while the man walked the potatoes, because she did not want to wet her knees. The woman screamed, while the fox swerved and the man tried to hit him with No. 5 shot at a range of ninety-five yards. . . .

When the man and woman had gone String Lug came out of the wood, his liking for the potato drills unchanged and his fear quite gone. He pushed into the thick growth with little hope of finding birds, but almost at once winded a pheasant with blood smell heavy upon it. The bird was a strong runner, with a wing fractured at the thumb, and he made good speed up the drills. String Lug allowed him to scramble clear of the potatoes, and caught him in the stubble when he trod on his dragging wing and fell with it buckled under him. He left with the bird in his jaws, and a half-notion in his head that his good fortune was due to the man with the gun.

That half-notion did not become full realization till some time later; but before he learned to play retriever— unasked, unwanted, and unseen—he had his first experience of the impact of war changes on a fox with a pre-war outlook.

On a moonless night, when the air was clammy chill with settling frost, he left Laverock Knowe on a poultry foray. He wanted easy prey, having gone to bed hungry that morning after stripping the tendons from a hare leg dry as a stick. He wasted no time seeking scents, for his mind was set on poultry. Crossing pasture, stubble and ploughland at a brisk trot, with the wind on the side of his face, he did not stop till he reached the potato pits near the road at Hackamore Farm. He halted because he heard the soft thud of footsteps in the lane. The salty tang of the air at the pits annoyed his sensitive nostrils, but he stood like a heron till the footsteps died away. A roe was pulling at a wheatstack by the road when he ducked under the hedge into the gloom of the Hackamore stackyard.

The crowded stacks made the air warm, and it smelt sweet to the fox's nostrils. String Lug walked with noiseless tread over a thick cushion of straw. Rats were scurrying about as they gathered grain. The farmyard was dark, the windows were dark, and everything was quiet except for the occasional stamp of a horse in its stall or the rattle of a cow chain in the byre. The tap by the stable door hissed its futile demand for a new washer. At the threshing shed gable String Lug sniffed critically and grinned when his nose found hens round the corner. Lint and Lassie barked when he turned the corner, but he heeded them not at all. Dogs often barked when no fox prowled, and String Lug knew that heavy-sleeping farmers rarely heard when collies raged in the night.

But this time all was changed. Before he reached the cart shed, where brown hens roosted unseen in the gloom, the doors of house and byre opened and twin shafts of light crossed in the yard. String Lug turned at the noise of opening doors and crouched, startled, at the lights. The lights went off when booted feet clattered on stone. McLeod reached the corner, carrying a torch, and another light stabbed the gloom. The fox's eyes flamed crimson in the beam, momentarily; then he was gone, a silent barghaist floating over the ground in snaking curves, held in the torchlight by McLeod till he could see the shape no more.

So String Lug was introduced to the "Black Out", an institution which made obsolete all his previous ideas about lights and bedtime. Not that he learned the whole truth at the first lesson. At first he treated it merely as an accident of timing. But two more visits to farms, at later dates and later hours, made him change his mind. And a raid on Mossrigg, when he was chased across the fields by Gallacher's Nell, convinced him that the new arrangement of darkened farms and waking men had come to stay.

That night he nursed a cut shoulder, for he fought with Nell for two minutes at the top of a field before she drew back with nipped pads and bleeding face, and allowed him to go. It was a confession by the big-hearted little sheep-dog that she was unable to handle such a big fox alone. Though he knew he was no longer being followed, String Lug forked his trail in case she should change her mind, or come back with Glen to pick up his line. He had no exaggerated ideas about fighting with two dogs simply because he had routed one bitch on ground which suited him and in light which was his own.

He slept, after the fight, through six hours of hunting darkness, and came out with a stiff shoulder when the sky was violet and the stars pale in the light of a newly risen crescent moon. Quartering the wood while the moon crossed the sky, he caught only a small vole in a ditch before the first gulls flew overhead in the dawn.

At ten o'clock in the morning he was lying inside the Brockhurst dyke near the cattle trough, licking his shoulder, catching the sun, sulky and cross with hunger. Out of the sun the air was crisp and pungent. Behind String Lug stood a beefy oak, with bracket fungus under its armpits, where a pinched wasp whined away the last hours of its life in the rays of the sun.

Cushats suddenly rose from the high ground and String Lug watched because he knew they had been disturbed. They flew swift and straight for the wood and he could hear the clatter of their wings when they pitched in the trees. Still farther out pheasants rose to the rumble of gunfire—five shots in all, then silence. String Lug pricked his ear. Minutes passed, while he took hasty licks at his shoulder. Then far off he heard the voices of men, without understanding a single word of their shouted conversation. "That one'll drop far out: send the dogs. . . .

Naw; send the bitch; this is *her* show . . . an' keep that ither eejit tae heel." And so on. But it was all noise to String Lug.

Then suddenly it happened. Over a collapsed part of the dyke, right in front of his nose, stumbled an old cock pheasant, spurred like a game cock, in all the fiery glory of his October plumage. He was badly shot in the shoulder, with one wing trailing. String Lug could hardly believe his eyes. But he did not doubt them long when his nose confirmed his sight. The bird stumbled right past his nose, and squatted flat at the base of the oak tree.

String Lug panted, and his breath was like white mist on the air. Then he moved like a striking viper. The noisy *chop-click* of his teeth was followed by a short scuffle, and the pheasant was limp in his jaws. He picked the bird up by the neck, dropped it again like lightning and spun round when he heard movement on the dyke. Coming over, right in the bird's tracks, was Jock Simpson's Labrador bitch. She stopped dead at sight of the fox, sniffing the musky air distastefully.

For fully a minute dog and fox stood rigid, face to face. The Labrador's hackles rose, but she neither growled nor showed her teeth. String Lug waited, liberally displaying ivory, with his eyes narrowed and his shoulders tight. Sensing that the dog's hesitation was due to fear, he was prepared to dispute to the point of fighting. The bitch sniffed in the direction of the pheasant, fidgeted, whined, pointed. . . . Her tail went down between her legs and under her belly in a curve like a question-mark. Instinct and training urged her to go for the pheasant; but fox fear kept her at her distance. Fighting was out of her line. And this was a big fox, with courage to match her own. So she turned and bolted, while String Lug snatched up the pheasant and raced to the gully beside the cattle trough.

Three men met the dog a hundred yards from the dyke.

The shooting tenant looked glumly at his friend, and Jock Simpson, scratching his head, looked curiously at the dog. A wild red setter scampered round the dejected bitch till she chopped at his jowl.

"There's a thing wrang here," said Jock quietly.

"Try the setter," said the shooting tenant's friend, who carried binoculars as well as a gun.

"Try it if ye like," Jock answered without enthusiasm, eyeing the sleek, hare-brained dog. "Every bird in that bag o' yours there was a runner, an' she got them a'. This is the first she's ever missed. There's a thing wrang!" Then suddenly, as a fox climbed out of the gully on their right, he shouted: "Gi'e me they field-glasses, quick!"

In a moment he had the powerful 10 x 50 glasses on the fox, and laughed. "There goes your phaisant, mister. I ken that fox," he added excitedly. "Damned if it isna goin' in for retrievin' noo. There's a chance for your setter. . . ."

But the setter could not be induced to go; nor could it be made to see the fox. The shooting tenant and his friend both watched String Lug through the glasses and saw that he really had the pheasant. But they were too polite to voice their disbelief in Jock's assertion that the fox was an old acquaintance. . . .

String Lug squatted on his belly beside a hole in the bank at the Laverock Knowe fence near his den. In the hole was a big buck rabbit which he had coursed from the field, and which had reached the hole with his teeth plucking the wool from its rump. The hole was not deep, as he could tell from the strength of the rabbit smell, and he was considering digging down for it. With one rabbit already in his burrow, he would not be hungry till another daylight had passed; but he was in provident mood and knew that the rabbit could not get away. So he set to work.

In fifteen minutes he had enlarged the burrow sufficiently to let all of him in except his brush. When he
withdrew his head to get his wind back he stood thigh-
deep in the soil he had scooped out. He cleared it by
standing over it and sending it under his belly in a shower
with his forepaws. Then he rested, panting, with dirt-
covered tongue hanging over his teeth. When he went back
to work again he discovered he could no longer dig standing up; so he lay down to it instead.

Lying on one side then the other, he pawed with
quick, short strokes which piled up the dirt against his
cheek. Every few minutes he wriggled out backwards,
pulling the loose stuff after him with his forepaws, and
becoming more and more excited as he neared the rabbit.
When he had worked in to his full length, including his
tail, his nose was six inches from the cowering rabbit. He
tried to snatch it, but the hole was too narrow and too
choked with loose soil. The click of his teeth when he
snatched could be heard ten paces away.

With the last of the obstructing soil removed, he went
back in for the kill. When he backed out the rabbit was
still alive and rolling its eyes, but one chop crushed its
spine and pierced its heart. Without pausing to shake the
soilings from his coat, he raced back to his den under the
scaur and laid the rabbit beside the one already there.
Only then did he take time to lick his fur and paw the
sand from his eyebrows.

Before the sun was yet due he dawdled through the
gloom of Mossrigg and went down to the burn to lap
water. The ground was soggy and the mud blistered up
between his toes at every step. At sunrise he was curled up
beside the big oak at the Brockhurst dyke, a spot he often
chose to catch the sun in the early morning. The big
field, still green with foggage, was dark and mist-swept.
The air was damp and raw, but there was no wind.

Presently the first cock pheasant crowed in the wood,

calling on hens roosting on one leg in larches with beaks pressed into shoulders. String Lug heard the loud whir of his wings, his harsh call as he touched down in the field, and could follow his outward course by his voice although he could not see him. Other cocks followed at intervals; then the hens came out clucking and stuttering. All of them started to feed, spectral, colourless shapes in the gloaming. The mist changed from grey to white as the sun topped the horizon. Overhead, the swish and whistle of wings as rooks flew to meet the sun: in the trees the twittering of small birds querying the time while they shook out cold from feathers. The sun's rays reddened the pines, a magpie *chuck-ucked*, and the whole world was awake.

Seven great swans flew overhead, whoopers with voices like golden trumpets, snow-plumaged travellers from the far north who knew the glacial winds of the tundra and the sun-drenched waters of Andalusia. The sun gilded the snow of their heads as they swept across the blue arch of sky; then they were gone, with a far-carrying swoosh of wings. They had passed over a Glasgow suburb only fifteen minutes before, flying high and strong in the familiar cold, unheard, unseen, eager to splash and dip their beaks in the cold water of the loch beyond Laverock Knowe.

String Lug stretched out as the sun warmed and the mist over the field billowed and drifted and disintegrated. The sheet of water in a hollow shone silver and mirrored every passing bird. Cushats came down out of the sun with clap and whistle of wings, followed by clamorous gulls which settled round the water in a heaving cloud. String Lug heard the next visitors before he saw them. *Tu-tu-tui* they called in flawless, liquid notes. They came out over the trees and wheeled in front of him, half a hundred strong, the first golden plover of the season, following the edge of winter southwards.

Christmas came with moonlit nights and skin-deep frost, and daisies still bravely opening petals in the winter sun. A flock of waxwings arrived, followed by snow buntings on their southward flight. For two days they fed on the berries of yew and thorn, bramble and brier; and then they were gone. On the morning they left, String Lug saw an old fox staggering drunkenly across a stubble field near Mossrigg Farm, and fled because he knew it had been wounded by gunshot and might be followed by dogs. The fox lingered for some days, feeding on a braxie sheep in the burn; and when it died it had contracted red mange, which is the scourge of weakly foxes.

Morning after morning, when String Lug crossed the big hayfield at Brockhurst, he saw pheasants feeding close to a corn stack by the roadside gate. Pigeons fed there too, rising only when road-users looked over the hedge. String Lug soon appreciated the possibilities of the stack, seeing it simply as a great stook where he could play the waiting game he had already played at two harvests. So one morning, when the full moon, three hours risen, shone brightly in a sky of snowflake clouds, he slipped under the supporting trestles of the stack and settled down to wait for pheasants.

The moon paled as the sun rose. In the east the sky turned pink and yellow and apple green. Overhead it brightened to the colour of a thrush's egg. Pheasants *cu-cupped* in the wood and String Lug cocked his ear. He was engrossed in watching birds drinking from a rain pool fifty yards away near the hedge when the pheasants left the wood behind him. Before the first of them came anywhere near the stack a peewit curled down to the pool, poked under its wings with its beak, and started to bathe. It stood belly deep and shook the water into spray with its wings. When it came out—leggy, skinny and dripping water—it ran its beak along its flight feathers, rubbed its ear on its shoulder and shook itself nearly off its feet. Then it went back in to bathe again. Just then String Lug saw a weasel in the hedge bottom, crouching among the withered stems of thistle, dock and knapweed.

The weasel had a plan—to catch the peewit while it was smothered in its own spray. String Lug guessed the plan and grinned his appreciation. In fact, he was already considering whether to step in and take the bird from the weasel when it had been caught. But the peewit lived to bathe on other days. The weasel pounced; Pica yattered a warning, and the bather leaped into the air on soaking wings. The weasel snarled and jabbered in rage, and returned to his mouseholes in the hedge bottom.

Not long afterwards String Lug heard the scrape of claws in straw and the pounding of hungry beaks on firm ground. The pheasants were pecking and scratching on the field side of the stack, with only a hedge thickness of packed stooks between them and the crouching fox. String Lug flexed his brush and gathered his hind legs in readiness. A green-and-crimson head appeared in the inverted V opening. The pheasant picked up an ear of corn and scratched its ear with a foot. It was the last grain it picked and the last time it scratched its ear. String Lug caught it while it had still one foot at its face. It screeched raucously when he chopped, and he had to close his eyes while its wings whipped his face in lightning beats which stung him to anger.

He was wise enough not to visit the stack during the next two days, knowing that the birds would shun it completely if they were continually ambushed. They did shun it after ten days, by which time he had taken three pheasants and one cushat. On his sixth visit he waited in vain, without being convinced they had really deserted the place. When he made his seventh call he was ambushed himself by Colin McLeod, and made up his mind to leave it alone afterwards whether the birds came back or not. McLeod had seen him leave the stack the previous morning, and hid under the trestles with his gun, believing the fox would come again. If String Lug had not come up with the utmost caution he would have been blown apart in the frosty morning. As it was, he got one pellet in his rump, and lost a wisp of fur from his flank, before he whisked out of the shotgun's range.

The pellet in his rump worried him little and he scraped it out with his teeth the following day. But the incident cooled his ardour for corn stacks and prompted him to try safer, if more arduous, forms of hunting. So he killed rats and rabbits, and chopped a weasel when it poked its head out of a field drain. Then he tired of fur, and longed for feathered prey, without thinking immediately of henhouses.

# Chapter Twelve

## "SCARFACE"

---

$S$TRING LUG CAME INTO GLENALDER ONE MORNING WITH a belly two days hungry, rime on his whiskers, and a pellet of No. 4 shot in his brisket. Pawing down a hen in a field beyond Skeoch, he had been surprised by a man with a gun as he was about to chop, and bolted without trying to get a mouth-hold on the bird. That sudden decision, together with his swerving run, saved his life, and only one pellet punctured his skin, at extreme range. Leg-weary though he was with much travelling on hard, frost-powdered ground, and irked by the smart of the pellet, he was too famished either to sleep or pause to scrape out the annoyance with his teeth.

On the wood edge, near the hollow where he had loafed so much in the days when the sun was warm, he heard the yarring of crows and the needling *tchock-ick-tlick* of magpies, and guessed that the birds were squabbling. Food being the likeliest cause of discord, he went to see. Two crows and two magpies flew to the safety of birch tops when he appeared in the open, and showered down abuse when he approached their feeding-place. Laid out neatly and evenly was a spread of minced rabbit gut with an enticing smell, and nearby lay a hen's gizzard shining like petrol stains on a rain-wet road. String Lug wanted to eat, and his mouth dripped saliva to urge him, but he did not like the layout and left it to the birds.

A few hundred yards away, under the beeches, he found the bodies of half a dozen magpies, lying close together on the frosted, russet leaf carpet. The birds' necks were pouchy, their crops puffy, and their talons clenched. String Lug turned up his snout and sidled away. He knew

143

the birds were not for him. Though he guessed they had been poisoned, it is doubtful if he connected them with John Long's doctored rabbit gut. In a vile temper at seeing so much food which he dared not touch, he walked slowly down the other side of the wood towards his burrow. Just when he thought he would have to go to bed hungry a sparrow-hawk provided him with a chittering bite to take the edge off his appetite.

The bird rose from a dead cushat on which she had been feeding. Unable to carry the heavy prey to a branch, she had been forced to make her meal on the ground. When String Lug took possession of the bird she had scraped the keel clean and was pecking at the skull, with the contents of the crop scattered round her on the grass. String Lug snatched up the body and raced to his den, leaving over a thousand grains of wheat and some sticky feathers behind. Mice fed on the wheat for many days afterwards, and Greywing, lean with famine, fed on the mice.

Six inches of snow fell and froze, and the east wind's icy talons raked the fur and feathers of the hunting clans. Real hunger came to the moor, hunger of the kind that stabs like a knife and kills in sleep. The berry-eating birds fared best, and ate snow because there was no water to drink. Black-game thronged the alders and birches to cram their crops with catkins, and the red grouse were never starving so long as the ling tips thrust above the snow. But owls died on their perches because mice and voles had vanished, and kestrels were reduced to feathers and bones.

While stoats packed and hares fled String Lug hunted alone, lean, savage, and reduced to eating scraps in farm middens. One day he saw three rabbits in a field, appearing hindquarters first, apparently out of the snow, disappearing and reappearing, again and again. Knowing there were no burrows at the spot, he began to stalk them warily, rushing forward when they disappeared and crouching motionless when they bobbed, fud foremost, above the snow. They were digging down to the grass and scraping up the snow to form a hollow. Each time they appeared on top they were scooping it up in their forepaws. String Lug killed one, and narrowly missed another; but the rabbits never came back to the hole which had proved a death-trap.

The rabbit lasted him for two days, during which he rarely left his burrow. On the third day he tried to run down a roe fawn sapling in the wood. He knocked the fawn out of her stride and reached her neck with his teeth, but he failed to hold her or roll her over and was thrown heavily to the ground with the tantalizing taste of blood on his tongue. That night he joined up with a small vixen from the northern woods and they hunted together, thus copying the greyhound foxes of the mountains whose blood ran in both their veins. In very hard weather the foxes on String Lug's range sometimes hunted in couples which were usually mated pairs, for in most winters the hardest weather came with the season of mating. But String Lug took to hunting with a vixen who was not his mate.

John Long saw them together, running into Glenalder, when he stopped beside the wood, on the road, the following day. The thaw which had begun in the night had glazed the snow crust and thinned down the ice on the pools and ditches to a creaking wafer. Long's spaniel jumped the ditch while he stood watching the foxes, and disturbed a greyhen feeding in a birch tree. The bird launched away in fright and Long's gun spoke when it crossed his front. It was a snap shot, with cold fingers fumbling at triggers, and the keeper was certain he had missed; but the dog had other ideas and galloped away in wild pursuit, heedless of the angry shouts of his master. When the dog came back from his quarter-mile run he was clouted with the gun barrels and chained to his master's waist. Then the keeper left to try elsewhere.

But the greyhen had not escaped the spreading shot. It had been hit in the neck and its wound was mortal, though it sped in unwavering flight for nearly five hundred yards before it fell like a stone into the big ditch on the Glenalder side of the road. The greyhen broke the ice, and floated in five feet of black, peaty water in a hole the size of its body, with its twisted wings spread on the surrounding ice wafer. All day it lay there, and when the frost settled down again at night, more savage than ever, the body was completely frozen in. By moonrise it was gripped in ice nearly a quarter of an inch in thickness.

In Glenalder Wood String Lug communed with his hunting partner. They were hungrier than spring hedgehogs. String Lug had seen Long's spaniel returning emptymouthed after the firing of the shot and, though he hadn't seen the bird fall, he knew from experience that the dog had been seeking lost game. So he contrived to persuade the vixen that the roadside ditch was the place for both of them on that moonlit, freezing night.

When the Dog Star, flaming green and crimson, had risen above the haze in the southern sky, they set off together across the frozen snow, making the merest whisper of sound with their pads and leaving only nail marks to betray their route. For more than an hour they cast about in narrowing circles where the spaniel had been ranging. Then String Lug found the bird, and barked his discovery to the vixen. She sniffed at the greyhen and at once became difficult, showing her teeth to warn String Lug that the prize was hers. When he moved forward tentatively to nose the bird she tried to rake his face, so he jumped aside because she was a vixen and already showing signs of the luring scent of mating. She was glad, however, to let him have a look when she discovered the bird was gripped in the ice, and String Lug saw at once what was needed.

He set to work with his nails on the ice, ripping off a

few feathers from the greyhen in the process, which the vixen tasted, then spat out because they were fleshless. With the bird partly freed, and water oozing through on one side, String Lug paused and pushed his nose into the wind. The scent he found there was elusive and faint, but he knew the taint because it was not unlike his own. In a moment he recognized the pebble-tapping chatter of hunting stoats, and savoured the full reek of their musky smell.

There were seven stoats in the pack, in full winter garb of white, with black-tipped tails. String Lug fell back a few paces, with his eyes flaming crimson hate. With hunger feeding courage he was determined to fight them off. They would not fall out over this bird! With the vixen by his side, he felt the odds were favourable. He hated stoats. He held that all stoats should be dead. And he meant to do executioner. . . .

And so, in the deceitful moonlight, a weird battle started. Two foxes, dancing and snapping, fought seven blood-thirsty, incredibly savage miniature tigers. The speed was little less than lightning. Fangs clicked and snaky bodies were tossed into the air. The stoats tissed like spitting cats and tapped out their war-cry as they fought in blind fury. The foxes were winning, but both of them had bleeding heels before five of the stoats were dead. One of the remaining two fled, but the seventh gripped the vixen by the big tendon of her right hind leg, and would certainly have ham-strung her had not String Lug bitten him almost in two.

Without stopping to lick their pads, the foxes returned to the greyhen and in a short time had the body out. The vixen snatched up the bird, snarled, wheeled, climbed almost out of the ditch, and recoiled when she found herself face to face with a small mongrel terrier the colour of an otter. Returning to his home at the loch after a long, fruitless vigil at a farm where a collie bitch was securely shut away from his unwanted attentions, he had heard the scuffling in the ditch and got the foxes' wind. Full of fight, and quite inexperienced, he had rushed to the worry.

Lithe and supple as a weasel, the vixen doubled back, with the growling dog at her throat. She dropped her bird and fell into the ditch, with the terrier straddling her and his teeth meeting in the side of her neck. When String Lug rushed to his partner's assistance the dog ignored him, for he was trying to chew inwards for a throat hold. That was his undoing. String Lug nipped all four of his pads, then slashed him again and again above the hocks till he almost severed his tendons. In the struggle dog and vixen fell into the pool which String Lug had made in the ice, with the dog underneath. More ice broke off with the weight so that the dog was almost immersed in the water. The shock, and the anguish in feet and legs, made him loosen his grip, and the vixen stumbled away, shaking her head.

String Lug pounced on the dog and tried to paw him under the water. Once the dog lost his nail grip on the ice and disappeared for a moment; then he bobbed up again and secured another hold. His powerful jaws kept chopping at the fox while he scrambled out, and String Lug wisely kept out of their reach. But when the dog bolted, staggering drunkenly with his hind legs almost buckling under him, he followed him some distance along the road, ripping and cutting with his teeth till the fugitive was screeching for mercy.

In the ditch the vixen still stood shaking her head. She was badly mauled, but not mortally wounded. Blood dripped from her neck and stained the snow. String Lug nudged her with his nose, but she turned away and climbed out of the ditch. For a few paces he followed her meekly, then he stopped, turned, and went back for the bird. If the vixen was going to bed to nurse a torn neck, he was not going to bed to nurse an empty stomach. And he not only carried away the greyhen. During the night he made two more journeys, and carried six stoats back to his den. The vixen was glad of his foresight afterwards, when hunger again troubled her more than her wounds; but she was quite ungracious because he had eaten the bird himself and left the tough, rubber and whipcord stoats for her.

At the turn of the year the little scar-faced vixen became String Lug's mate. Three feet of soft snow lay on the moor. In the fields it lay fence deep, and in the moonlight the stob tops looked liked black pencil-ticks on white paper. Grouse fed where the sheep trod out the snow, but the foxes went hungry and had to lie up till the frost came again to save them from floundering belly deep. On the first night of easy walking they caught a September-born leveret while it slept in a snowdrift where it had been lying for days. Once they caught a grouse in a crude burrow on the moor. But poultry was hard to come by, rabbits were few, and even the rats in the farmyards stayed under cover.

String Lug crossed the moor when the moon was full, leaving Scarface, the vixen, chewing at fern stools in Glenalder. The stars were brilliant and the cold intense. A roebuck, wearing only one horn, rose to his feet and walked away stiffly when he saw the fox against the snow. The beast was sickening with fluke, the embryo of which he had picked up on a grass blade, where it had climbed and grown a horny skin, after escaping from the body of a snail. Turning to look after the roe, String Lug smelt grouse on the wind, and flattened instantly, almost merging with his shadow. With the birds' position carefully plotted with his nose, he went into the stalk.

Suddenly a grouse chuckled throatily, questioningly, and three others, sheltering in holes in the snow, raised heads to listen. Eyes blinked and ears strained, and presently the heads went down again. Once more the first grouse chuckled, and again they were all long-necking to see what was afoot. This time they felt uneasy. Croupy and cold and hungry they were; but they were not stupid. That whispering sound as of a dragon-fly's rubbed wings was not imagination: it was the scrape of pads on frozen snow. One beak opened and called *ho-a-ack*, and three grouse rose with whir and jingle of wings as String Lug rushed the caller. And the caller died while its breath vaporized on the frosty air.

The bird was emaciated and String Lug ate it on the spot without showing it on his flanks, which were lean and rib-taut with hunger. At Firknowe spinney he met Scarface. Together they trotted to the stackyard at the farm, with ice crystals hanging from their belly and brush fur, and tinkling like fairy bells.

Running through the stackyard was a lone dog otter, rudder pencilling the snow and fur gleaming oilily in the moonshine. String Lug smelt *man* in the yard and back-tracked with Scarface into the shadow of the stacks. Circling the danger area, they picked up the otter's trail and followed it to the loch. The man under the tarpaulin by the woodpile sat with gun on knees, chilled and chittering, waiting for grey geese coming in to pull corn from stacks—geese which would not come that night because they had fed elsewhere. And he knew nothing of the passing of the otter, nor of the foxes which were following him down to the frozen loch.

The otter was after ducks. So were the foxes. Ducks were the answer to all their problems. When the loch froze there were always callers on the sleeping ducks, eager to drink the birds' hot blood and so warm their own. For the hunters of the wild learn quickly. And the loch which was the ducks' refuge from peril was to-night a right of way for their enemies. The foxes reached the high peat bank, frozen and snow-crusted, and scanned the ice. The cold was savage and penetrating and the moon looked sardonically down.

Scarface and String Lug nosed the wind. They could smell the otter, and the ducks and geese beyond. The bank shadow cast by the moon hid the birds; but it also hid the otter. Not a grey goose of the seven sensed his coming; the ducks slept on one leg, with beaks pressed into shoulders, unaware of the peril on the ice. The foxes followed in the wake of the otter, crouching low and hugging the bank shadow. Suddenly the otter streaked across a neck of moonlight. His rush was swift, accurate, deadly. Wings hummed and swished; webbed feet slapped the ice; and geese and ducks were in the air in a milling throng, clamorous and terrified, beating up into the face of the moon in a ragged circus. A duck flapped on the ice, and the otter tasted blood.

Patter of pads on ice and the two foxes closed in a converging attack on the otter, snapping with clash of ivory fangs as the jaws of the duck-killer opened to display still sharper teeth. The foxes snarled and the otter nickered. His lack-lustre eyes glimmed fierce, and his whiskers twitched. But what is one otter against two hungry foxes, Scottish hill foxes at that, lean and hard-bitten, with empty bellies and hearts full of fight?

Oh, he was dour, that otter, straddling his duck and ready to fight. They bit him. They chopped and cut him, and walloped him across the face with their brushes. He made them sneeze blood as they breinged at him; but if they were sneezing blood he was beginning to ooze it. So he quit, and slithered away across the ice in a rage. And the foxes pounced on the duck—a fat mallard with a punctured heart.

Scarface ate first because her stomach was empty. Afterwards they parted company for the night. On his way back to Glenalder String Lug chopped a weasel, a lean female fierce with famine, which he hid under a peat

151

overhang in case he should want it later. But Greywing saw him hide it; and Greywing was lean with fasting. So he pulled out the weasel with his great fish-hooks of claws and ate part of it ravenously, ripping off mouthfuls of corded muscle with his powerful beak. He carried the remainder to his roost to be devoured on the morrow. It was the first time he had ever eaten food not killed by himself.

The thaw came at last and String Lug caught no more ducks when the thinning loch ice creaked and fractured under his weight. Lean hunting was still the rule, for the snow melted slowly. Rabbits in low burrows were drowned by the drain of water. Daily, String Lug saw corn-stacks in fields black with rooks, and grey with cushats. Hares came to the farmyards in the night to nibble hay and swedes, leaving when the cushats flapped down to the wheat-stacks in the dawn.

String Lug hunted on with his mate through the long, bitter, starlit nights, when even the stoats had gone; but one day he, too, felt the urge to move.

Almost inevitably his trail led to the warm woods and fat farmlands of his old range. Scarface joined him without argument, for she was glad to quit the famine-stricken moor, and had no prejudices about the direction to be taken. In the small hours of the morning, in slushy snow, and with a raw, blustering wind in their faces, they left Glenalder, following the route String Lug had taken more than two years before after his brief sojourn on the moor. They nosed scents and followed trails on the way, but all they had to eat was some thaw-soggy pig-food in a trough by the roadside, opposite a farm. At break of day, with sleet driving in from the west, they entered Laverock Knowe Wood, which was eleven miles from Glenalder in a direct line, but almost twenty in the tracks of the foxes.

Jock Simpson crossed String Lug's trail a few days after

OH, HE WAS DOUR, THAT OTTER

his return and, though not the first to see him, was the first to recognize him. He announced the fact with due ceremony in the Mossrigg Farm kitchen the same night.

"The grey fox wi' the lug is back fae the deid," he told the rabbit-catcher and Gallacher. "I ran into him this mornin'."

Both men were incredulous. "Ye must be mistook!" said Tamson scoffingly.

"Listen," said Jock. "This mornin' I saw a fox runnin' across the lane at Laverock Knowe Ferm wi' something in his mooth that looked like string. In the haidge bottom, where the fox rose, was a haidgehug. . . ."

"Hedgehug!" exclaimed the moocher. "At this time o' year? They're sleepin', man!"

"This wan deed in its sleep!" retorted Jock. "The fox dug it oot an' it was the haidgehug's inside he was trailin' in his gub! An' it was the grey fox a' right. I could never mistake that lug or hide in a million years!"

"That's mebbe the same fox," said Gallacher suddenly.

"Whit same fox?" the others asked almost together.

Gallacher pushed his cap back over his grizzled hair as he explained. That morning he had seen his hens pecking at something near a stack where a snare had been set for a hare. Thinking they were pecking at the snared hare he had hurried out to collect it; but when he arrived it was a fox that ran away. He had been eating the hare.

"That settles it," said the moocher. "That bliddy fox spent a' his spare time emptyin' ma snares. If he thinks he's gaun tae start . . . But d'ye mean tae say your hens was pickin' at a fox?"

"They were peckin' at something," replied Gallacher.

"It's likely enough when ye think o' it," Jock said, rubbing his chin. "Nell an' Glen get nae peace wi' the hens pickin' their tails every time they lie doon, an' the hens maybe thocht the fox was a dug, them no bein' able to smell. An' nae fox wi' ony sense wid start a clatter among hens when he was havin' a gran' feed o' hare, 'specially when he could have a hen for the takin' when he was through!"

Gallacher guffawed, but was convinced Jock's reasoning was sound. "I weesh some bodies had as muckle gumption," he said. "Ah weel; a wee bit mair hell aboot the place'll no make ony great odds."

# Chapter Thirteen

## THE FOX-SHOOT

CUSHATS WERE BROODING FIRST CLUTCHES IN FLIMSY nests when Scarface whelped in Laverock Knowe, in the narrowest, deepest part of the glen. There was skin-deep frost, with a heavy cranreuch, when her cubs were born. Tufter, the long-eared owl, roosting on the wood edge, saw the vixen leave her rock hole a dozen times during the day—heavy-eyed, nervous, bedraggled, and pinched about the hindquarters. The owl's mate had been sitting for nearly three weeks on five glossy white eggs under a washed-out tree root in the wood, and he was perturbed at the arrival of such a dangerous neighbour so near his lowly home.

Five cubs were born to Scarface in the rock hole in the glen. When she came out after the birth of the last one, to chew grass and fibre, she was skinny and waspish of waist, and a very sick fox. For forty-eight hours afterwards she was still a very sick fox, drinking much water, but eating nothing at all; yet with an abundance of milk which kept her family sleeping and growing. The birth of her cubs had injured her delicate tissues—they were very big cubs and she was a very little vixen—and the cold had set up a dangerous inflammation. But, quite suddenly, she felt well again; her fever vanished; and she started to eat. During her illness String Lug had put down nine rats, two rabbits and a headless hen, and on these she started, with a ravening hunger she had not known since she left the moor.

String Lug saw her for the first time in three days when he followed Tufter into the wood at dawn. The fox was carrying two rats in his jaws and the owl had one in his talons. All three had been lifted from Hackamore Farm. Pigeons *croo-crooed* in the trees with more assurance than hitherto, for the frost had gone and the first wood anemones were unfolding in the wood. String Lug pressed new tracks in the loam, and double-printed old ones softened in the thaw. Scarface showed no interest in the rats because she still had nine of them and a rabbit and a half. She had eaten the hen first when she regained her appetite. Milk oozed from her nipples when she hurried back to her nursery, after chewing playfully at her mate's jowl while he stood looking foolish with his mouth stuffed with rats.

That night a strong wind blew from the west, and high-sailing vapour clouds blurred the racing moon. String Lug followed the hedge in the Hackamore wheatfield, while searchlights probed the sky, and stopped beside an ivy-covered oak tree when the rumble of gunfire came from afar. Far to the west he heard explosion after explosion, while the sky glowed red and searchlights criss-crossed where aircraft roared above the clouds. For a moment he was afraid, till he realized the gunfire was very far away. Then he found something of more immediate interest which made him close his ears to the uproar.

A stoat was climbing stealthily up the ivy of the oak to a bushy crotch where a scared cushat was sitting close on two white eggs. String Lug saw the stoat, but could only guess what it was after; so he waited to see, and to chop it when it came back to earth.

Higher and higher the stealthy hunter climbed, without disturbing a single ivy leaf. When it darted into the ivy-cushioned crotch it was smothered in wildly flapping wings, and a terrified cushat took the air. The bird flew heavily across the wheatfield and String Lug knew it had the stoat attached. Grinning because he knew the cushat was going to be his, he galloped across the field, keeping just below the heavy-flying bird, ready for the moment when it would relax like a rag and come pitching to earth.

When it did fall at last, just short of the burn, shedding feathers torn out by the stoat on the way, he met it as it hit the ground with a thud. The stoat's head was buried in the feathers of the bird's neck, and it died without ever seeing the fox. String Lug tossed the kicking body aside and picked up the cushat, which had its throat almost torn out and its breast feathers soaked with blood.

The noise of gunfire came more frequently when he was walking back to the glen with his cushat. In the big field before Laverock Knowe he met Bounce, the roebuck, bounding madly downhill, with two does crowding him from behind as he fled. String Lug watched the roe into Mossrigg Strip, then hurried to a heathery knoll in the glen which he had chosen as his seat, his look-out and his sleeping place. There he lay down to eat his bird. The gunfire and bomb explosions continued till an hour before daybreak, keeping the roosting pheasants *cu-cu-cupping* in alarm, and Tufter and Keewick from their hunting. String Lug pondered, but could not solve, the problem, and went to sleep when quiet returned.

That spring he killed more rats than he had ever caught in the same period before, in the stackyards, at the coup, and later in the hedge bottoms. They were big rats, and fat, but not the most sustaining of food, and the foxes had to eat many of them to satisfy a little hunger. But if rats were plentiful, rabbits were few. Much long-netting and shooting, to supply larders denuded by war, had thinned them out alarmingly, and most of those which String Lug saw sitting hunch-backed beside burrows were tiny youngsters of the year. Pheasants, too, had dwindled, for few were being reared by hand, and birds breeding wild had their eggs lifted by prowlers with wings, prowlers on two feet and on four. Hares were still plentiful and String Lug caught them when he could; but rats were the mainstay of his cubs when they were first weaned.

One night he killed a rat while it was dragging a naked baby rabbit from a hole in the Mossrigg scree. It was a big rat, a grandfather among rats, and it squealed like a pig at the grip of his teeth. Turning to leave with both rat and rabbit in his jaws, he noticed the wool entangled in the feet of the killer and clinging to the mouth of the hole. So he laid down his mouthful and started to dig, and was rewarded with five more naked baby rabbits cuddled up in a nest of fur pluckings at the end of the burrow.

By the time the first swallows were nesting and the early cushat flappers were losing their last thread-down in flight, Scarface's cubs were treading out runways among the bracken and birches in the glen, and wandering dangerously near the road at the top. String Lug, crossing one morning from the birches with a doe rabbit heavy in milk, met two of them among the tall heather by the roadside. He rushed at them angrily, snarling without dropping his rabbit, and they fled down to the den mouth with puppy tails curled under bellies.

Scarface, meeting her mate halfway down the slope, nosed his ear, took the rabbit, and hurried to her cubs with the hair of her spine on end. When the cubs mobbed her at the den she girned them down, and hustled them all roughly underground without letting them near the rabbit. For Scarface, like String Lug, was bent on teaching them to stay away from the road. String Lug sat grinning, with hanging tongue, till the cubs were safely out of sight, then went back to the birches to hunt for mice.

But more than one lesson was needed to keep the cubs away from the road. It had, for them, a seemingly irresistible fascination. Late one day, when the sun was low and peewits were weeping above the fields at Laverock Knowe Farm, a military car sped along the road just after one of the cubs had crossed. The cub lost his nerve when the car whined close, and shot back across the road when it was almost level. The driver knew he had hit something and stopped the car. When he walked back along the road he found the fox cub dead and rolled it over twice with his foot. Then he drove away, leaving the body on the road.

It was fortunate for the foxes that the cub had been killed by a car passing through, for no farmer was told and the soldier was travelling a long distance beyond. But a dead cub lying on the road would soon be connected with the glen by the first local passer-by. Whether or not Scarface sensed such a possibility, she dragged the mutilated body from the road, pawed and nosed it against a cushion of bracken in the glen, and scraped wet mould over it till it was almost completely hidden from sight. Later String Lug nosed the loose mound beside the bracken stool, and he, too, scraped earth upon it. Then both of them promptly forgot all about it, and never looked near it again.

Even with Scarface hunting, String Lug found his duties no less arduous, for he had to travel just as far each night on a range alarmingly depopulated of rabbits and game birds. The cubs fared better than before, because two foxes increased the food supply by doubling the distance travelled in hunting for it. String Lug and the vixen fed mostly on rats and mice and frogs and beetles, with an occasional young rabbit or plover, or a bird caught on its nest. But both of them soon began to crave more red-blooded prey.

In the eight weeks since the birth of his cubs String Lug had killed only four hens and two ducks, all carried many miles from farms beyond his usual range. But growing appetites were demanding greater food supplies and he took to killing hens more frequently. Feathers soon littered the ground beside the hole in the glen, but no farmers came seeking foxes, for all the birds had been carried from far away. String Lug was wise enough to pursue such a course as a matter of policy. But Scarface, knowing the immediate needs of her four cubs, and seeing so many flocks of poultry on range within easy carrying distance, took the shortest route to her prey and struck her first blow at Mossrigg. And she killed not one hen, but five. . . .

After that first night she ran riot through every farm in the neighbourhood, killing foraging hens in the day-light of early morning or when grain was scattered for them before roosting time. Yet the earth was not imme-diately discovered, for farmers were too busy increasing the yield of their acres to do other than take snap-shots at foxes as opportunity offered. Some of them tried lying in ambush in henhouses at dawn or dusk, but on these days Scarface usually killed elsewhere. Jock Simpson had been out of the district for some weeks, and was not yet due back; and Pate Tamson was seldom on the ground with snares or traps, because rabbits were few. So Scarface was not sought after by the two men most likely to find her.

When Jock Simpson did come home, every farmer was talking foxes; but before the fencer found the earth in the glen, Scarface's hen-killing days were over.

String Lug was trotting home with a grouse in his jaws when the anti-aircraft guns opened fire for the first time in nearly two months. The gunfire was much nearer than when he had last heard it, for new batteries were in action only a few miles from the glen. Again in the west he saw the glare of fire in the sky, and overhead the end-less criss-crossing of searchlights. In the distance he could hear the boom and rumble of exploding bombs, and the crack of quick-firing guns. Aircraft were roaring high in the sky behind him when he reached the roadside hedge above the glen at Laverock Knowe; and the bombs fell just as he was crossing.

The shock of the first shattering burst was sickening, and rocked him on his legs, for it had fallen only three hundred yards away at the end of the glen. Terrified, he clawed his way into a drain under the road, and lay trembling throughout the rest of the darkness. A second bomb fell in Hackamore wood, and a third on the road beyond, near the village. A few houses lost glass from windows and hens roosting in cabins near the road were killed by the third explosion. And String Lug, uninjured, felt only a little nervous in the morning. But when he found his mate she was lying dead near the crater at the end of the glen, killed by blast, unmarked, and with a dead rabbit still gripped between her clenched teeth.

Davidson and Gallacher found the dead vixen during the day when they came to examine the bomb crater; water was already draining into it and they saw at once the danger to cattle if it was not fenced off right away. String Lug, hiding in the wood, watched them walking about and wailed heart-brokenly when they carried the vixen's body away. Both men heard the cry, and knew its meaning, without guessing that the dog fox was within hailing distance of four cubs roystering beside a rock hole in the glen. It was only when Jock Simpson came, with Andrew from Laverock Knowe Farm, that the den was discovered. But that was some days later.

For an hour after the departure of the men String Lug wailed at five-minute intervals, while three long-eared owlets stared wonderingly from a tree. Bounce, browsing in the wood, heard it too, and came up close to inquire, and when String Lug finally left he saw the roebuck, with ears up, standing less than twenty yards away. Bounce fled and String Lug padded to the wood end to mourn in silence for the rest of the daylight.

At nightfall he returned to the den and permitted the

cubs, dancing on their hind legs, to paw his face and lick his ears. They knew nothing of their mother's death; nor were they apparently upset at her failure to come. String Lug, knowing they were yet a long way from being able to fend for themselves, was ready to take over the task of caring for them unaided.

The demands of his four motherless cubs taxed his powers and skill to the limit. From dusk till daylight, and sometimes well into the morning, he hunted tirelessly to keep them supplied. He met his responsibilities by running himself thin and feeding lean, except on nights of plenty, when he gorged till his ribs were taut. He brought moles and rats, mice and plover, a hare, two partridges and a duck, frogs, newts and dead chicks thrown out from brooders at farms. The duck he snatched from Gallacher's flock when the birds were swimming in the burn in Moss-rigg Strip, well out of sight of the farm.

During daylight he rarely left his watching place on the knoll, even when the cubs were below ground, for, contrary to popular belief, he took his duties as father very seriously indeed. The cubs now showed little inclination to play about in the middle of the day, and had completely given up stravaiging to the road. After the first fussing, when he had taken over the duties of father and mother, String Lug kept clear of their paws and tongues, and it was seldom indeed that they saw him, unless during the hours of darkness; even then he made a habit of dropping the prey, and barked for them to come and seek for it. One night they barked in reply, and he knew they were growing up fast; but in the morning he saw Jock Simpson at the den and knew that trouble lay ahead.

Without waiting for nightfall, he hustled the cubs into the heart of Laverock Knowe wood, where they lay, quiet and invisible as woodlice, during the day. At night, he led them across the fields and burn to Hackamore wood, and put them to bed in the old burrow he knew so well. Jock Simpson's discovery of the earth had prompted him to move; but the scent of Corrie on the doorstep later in the day decided him beyond all question. . . .

In the Mossrigg Farm kitchen, more than a week later, Jock Simpson was sitting at the big table with Gallacher and a stranger of middle age who was an evacuee from the Midlands of England.

"Take it fae me," Jock was saying to the Englishman, "your foxes are bits o' weans compared wi' oors. Oor beasts are fae the hill, man! An' that wan wi' the lug— he's the daddy! You'd never convince *him* this was Scotch!" He looked critically at his tot of Mossrigg whisky. "Man, sir," he said to Gallacher, "watter's a gran' drink when ye take it in the proper spirit!"

"But there's foxes and *foxes*," said the Englishman, leaning across the table.

"True," laughed Jock; "an' we've got the *foxes*!"

Gallacher winked to the Englishman. "But we've got oor stumors tae. Look at the wan I shote on the midden when it was dreamin', in broad daylicht!"

"That was an English evacuee fae Leecester," was the quick retort, and Gallacher's booming laugh almost shook the delft on the kitchen shelf.

At that moment the door opened and Pate Tamson came in. His pockets were bulging with nets and snares, but he had neither ferret nor rabbits.

"Hullo! Pate," Gallacher greeted him. "Nae rabbits yet?"

"Rabbits!" exclaimed the moocher. "I had wan in a snare, but that damned fox has whupped it awa! An', speakin' o' foxes, whit aboot the hole in the glen at Laverock Knowe?"

"Flitted!" replied Jock Simpson. "I've had Corrie in that hole three times in the last week jist tae make sure.

But there's nothing there noo. An' there's sae damn little time these days tae go lookin' efter foxes: they micht be onywhere!''

Two days afterwards Jock and Colin McLeod of Hackamore crossed the fields to examine the woodside fence. Their boots were drenched and glistening, and dotted with grass seed and buttercup petals. Colin suddenly gripped his companion by the arm and pointed along the woodside. Near the fence a fox cub was struggling in a snare.

The cub's left hind leg was bared to the bone in the grip of the noose and there was sweat foam on its lips. Jock caught it by the ruff and freed the leg from the strangle-hold of the wire. "Poor wee eejit!" he said, shaking his head. "Did your mither never learn ye better than that?"

"Some hare this!" he said to the amazed Colin. "I've kent a haidgehug walk into a snare often enough, but . . . well, we're aye learnin'.'' He became eloquent in his theorizing as he rolled over a very dead young rabbit with his foot. "See the bit rabbit his mither brocht him? An' see how this wire is splayed and keenked? That was a fox's teeth, man. An' the peg tae; chowed up, near through in fact. Anither ten meenits and the auld fox wid hae gotten him awa, trailin' a yaird o' wire. . . .''

"And what d'ye make o' that?" asked McLeod, pointing to the wing of a hen lying near the snare.

"Likely the cub wid be humphin' it, Colin. They dae that. Jist like a body's dochter leavin' hame an' takin' part o' the hoose wi' her!"

"It'll humph nae mair, then," said Colin. "Chap it on the heid!"

"Best take it to the ferm an' shoot it dacent," Jock answered quietly. "I'll carry it that far."

On the point of leaving, Colin spoke again. "D'ye think this cub micht hae come oot o' Hackamore?"

164

"It's likely enough, at that."

"Then we'll drive it the morn an' see what we get in the poke."

Next day was Saturday, and at two o'clock thirteen men, eight of them with guns, stood waiting for McLeod on the edge of the wood. At two-fifteen he arrived, riding bareback on a Clydesdale mare he was turning out to grass. "Here comes John Peel noo!" said Jock Simpson. "Where's your red coat an' your dugs, Colin?"

"Everybody here?" asked McLeod, dismounting. "Good! Awa wi' ye, wummin!" The mare jumped away when he slapped her on the rump. "Where's the dug?" he said to Jock.

"Robert's comin' wi' him. He'll be here directly."

The party was sorted out. The wood was to be driven by seven men, two of them carrying guns. Gallacher and McLeod each took a corner of the wood at the west end. The remaining four guns were posted on the flanks, two of them to walk fifty yards ahead of the line of beaters, and two to stand about the same distance from Gallacher and McLeod on the edge of the wood. Jock Simpson and the shooting tenant were to walk with the drivers in case a fox tried to squeeze back. The beaters were spread across the waist of the wood and started to move forward when Jock shouted: "Right!"

The men moved forward slowly, beating sticks, picking their way round boggy patches and ducking under tightly-laced, rotten fir branches. Twigs snapped underfoot and faces were blackened and scratched. Pigeons clattered from high nests at the disturbance; magpies chattered and scolded; and Keewick flapped away through the trees, affronted at the noise. A labourer on the right suddenly shouted that he had seen foxes ahead; almost in the same instant Jock saw String Lug rise from a tree root and skulk away among the bracken. "Get ready an' don't blink!" he shouted to the shooting tenant. "This fox is a warmer!"

For Jock was certain that the fox he had seen was his old friend with the lug.

Forty yards from the west end of Hackamore the men on the flanks began to close in to the wood. Gallacher and McLeod stood with guns ready on the corners. Then everything happened at once.

String Lug dashed into view, among the thinning trees —alone, streaking for the fence. He swerved as the flanking guns fired once, twice. . . . He wheeled and was racing back when Gallacher and McLeod opened up on him. His speed and the way he weaved round the tree trunks put them right off. Smoke drifted and men swore. The three cubs broke cover, piled through the fence, and were racing across the field before a single gun could be reloaded. Gallacher swore again. McLeod swore again. And String Lug fled back . . . back . . . faster than any sheepdog, in a bewildering series of swerves and spurts . . . through the line of beaters . . . flattening . . . zigzagging erratically as a mortally wounded cat. . . . The shooting tenant managed a single shot at him. He faltered for a moment when the gun roared, then disappeared into the undergrowth.

"I hit it!" shouted the shooting tenant. "It can't get far!"

Jock Simpson was certain that the fox was not badly hit, but he said nothing till Gallacher arrived, puffing and spluttering. "The auld fox is hit," Jock told him, "but, judgin' by the language, ye missed the cubs. . . ."

"Missed them!" Gallacher swallowed hard. "That bliddy fox drew a' the fire an' the cubs got clean awa! Twelve shotes fired at wan fox an' only some grass cut! It's a good job ye copped the auld fox, mister," he turned to the shooting tenant, "for the rest o' us couldna hit a barn!"

"It'll look for a quiet place to die: animals always do," said the shooting tenant sententiously.

"Then we'd better get started lookin' for the daith-bed!" It was Jock Simpson who spoke.

McLeod ran up shouting: "The cubs are in the whins awa doon the burn. They micht lie there a wee. . . ."

"You folks get awa, then, an' try again," said Jock, "an' I'll look for the auld yin. The dug'll be here ony time noo wi' Robert, an' if there's a wounded fox in the wid he winna miss it. If the fox is deid, I'll lug it in," he said to the shooting tenant.

The party left for the whins and Jock turned back alone through the wood, although he was still certain that the fox had only been clipped in a foot. Before he had gone fifty yards he met Robert with Corrie on a lead. Robert had one sleeve of his jacket pinned down, for he had lost an arm in the war.

"I heard the shooting," Robert greeted him. "Any luck?"

"Plenty foxes," Jock answered laughingly. "But they a' got awa. Ye didna see a fox on your way in?"

Robert shook his head while Corrie struggled to be free. Jock told him what had happened. The terrier was turned loose and both men followed at a run when he bolted away. Corrie was running String Lug's blood line.

"He's on tae something," Jock exclaimed excitedly, thumbing the hammers of his gun.

Near the bomb crater on the north flank of the wood they found Corrie running in circles, barking furiously, and obviously at a loss. Then he worked in to the splintered base of a tree which had been shattered in the explosion. The tree was lying at a low angle against another one which was also scarred and blasted. The terrier nosed the rough bark and was trying to run up the tree when Jock called him in. Lying on the pine needle clump, where the head of the fallen tree was resting on a thick branch of the other, was String Lug. He knew the terrier had found him; and he knew Jock Simpson could see

167

him. But there was no way out. To jump down meant breaking his neck, and at the bottom of the sloping tree was Corrie, with two men and a gun. So he sat still, quivering, thinking, hoping, while blood drip-dripped from his injured paw.

Jock raised his gun. "See that fox?" he said to Robert. "That's the wan ye saw among the moudie heaps afore ye jined the sodgers. An' look at that lug! Ye couldna mistake it in an army o' foxes. An' noo he's tichter caught than a rabbit in a snare!"

Robert saw, for the range was only twelve yards and the fox made no move to hide his head. String Lug, indeed, was sitting staring at them as though completely indifferent. When Jock put his eye to the gun barrels Robert spoke.

"Wait!" he said. "You've told me a lot about this fox, and how you can think of shooting a beast you once went to the trouble of saving as a cub. . . . Why not let him go?"

"Hens is hens, Robert lad, an' very precious in wartime. Thur foxes are killin' hens galore. Man, I don't like shootin' the beast for the sake o' shootin', like some folks. But killin' hens!"

"There's more than hens being killed right now," Robert persisted. Then, laughingly, he added: "Damn it, man, my arm was precious to me; but I lost it! What's a hen? Where's the sentimentalist about foxes now? That's your adopted son up there!"

Jock was slowly wavering. "But Gallacher wid go clean aff his heid. So wid Colin an' the rest. . . ."

"They would—if we told them! But we don't have to, and Corrie certainly won't. Anyway, they don't know whether the beast was hit or not!"

And suddenly Jock started laughing. Robert laughed. And Corrie barked because he thought something was going to be done at last with the fox up the tree. But he was led away through the wood, dancing and straining at the lead, while the fox watched and rose to his feet in his lofty seat. The men halted within view of the tree and saw String Lug pick his way down as gracefully as a cat. And when he had hirpled away, looking over his shoulder till he was hidden among the trees, Jock turned to Robert and said:

"They say there's a fool born every meenit; but here's wan that's been born twice!" And he pointed to himself.

# Glossary

| | |
|---|---|
| BARGHAIST | goblin in the shape of a large dog |
| BIRSES | bristles |
| BOSE | empty — hollow (as an empty barrel), hollow-sounding |
| BRACKEN | large, coarse fern |
| BRAXIE | diseased mutton |
| BREINGED | rushed wildly |
| BRISKET | breast of animal |
| BURN | brook |
| BUTT | shelter for guns during a grouse drive |
| BYRE | cowshed |
| | |
| CAVEY | cage or coop |
| CHOP | to snap with the jaws |
| CLEG | gadfly or horsefly |
| CLUTCH | setting of eggs |
| CORNCRAKE | a bird, also called land rail, which lives among mowing grass |
| COUP | rubbish heap, dump |
| CRANREUCH | hoarfrost |
| CRAW | crop |
| CROUSE | bold, lively |
| CUSHAT | wood pigeon, ringdove |
| | |
| DEID | dead |
| DIPPER | any of several diving birds, especially the water ouzel |
| DOUR | obstinate, sullen |
| DRY-STONE DYKE | stone wall without mortar |

| | |
|---|---|
| FENCER | fence maker |
| FIELDFARE | species of thrush which spends the winter in the British Isles |
| FLAPPER | young wild duck or partridge |
| FLUKE | parasitic worm |
| FUD | tail |
| GEAN | wild cherry tree |
| GIN | steel trap with jaws |
| GIRNING | snarling |
| GREYHEN | female black grouse |
| GURRYING | growling deep in the throat |
| HACKNEY | horse |
| HEADRIGG | top of a field where the plough turns |
| HOG-SHOUTHERED | charged shoulder to shoulder roughly |
| JOUKING ABOUT | dodging in and out |
| KNOWE | small hill |
| LEATHERJACKET | grub of the crane fly |
| LEVERET | young hare |
| LING | a kind of heather |
| LOCH | lake |
| LUG | ear |
| LURCHER | crossbred dog, a cross between collie and greyhound, used by poachers for catching rabbits |
| MICHT | might |
| MIDDEN | dunghill |
| MOOCHER | loafer |
| MOUDIE HEAPS | molehills |
| PIE | magpie |
| POP-HOLE | small hole in wall of henhouse |

| | |
|---|---|
| RICKLE | ramshackle pile |
| RIDE | path through woodland |
| RODE | to make a regular evening flight during the breeding season (woodcocks) |
| RUDDER | tail |
| RUTTING SEASON | mating season of deer |
| | |
| SCAUR | cliff, bank, ridge or hill |
| SCRAPE | place where the soil has been scraped up |
| SCREE | boulders and rocks and stones |
| SCREIGH | shriek |
| SETT | earth or burrow |
| SHILFA | chaffinch |
| SHOTE | shot |
| SLIDDER | one who walks in slouching fashion, dragging feet |
| SLUGHING | puffing |
| SMIRRING | drizzling |
| SNELL | keen, bitter, severe |
| SPATE | sudden flood caused by melting snow or heavy rain |
| SPEIR | enquire after or look for |
| SPINNEY | small wood or clump of trees |
| STACKYARD | yard where straw or grain is stacked |
| STOAT | ermine |
| STOB | fence post |
| STOOK | to set up sheaves in piles |
| STOOL | root |
| STUMOR | stupid person |
| SWEDE | turnip |
| | |
| TACKETS | hobnails |
| TATTIE PITS | trenches where potatoes are stored against frost |

| | |
|---|---|
| THREAD-DOWN | pinfeathers — down of young pigeons |
| TORMENTIL | herb used in medicine and in tanning |
| TOUSIE | rough, shaggy |
| | |
| WARMER | active and clever — tricky |
| WATER-VOLE | water rat |
| WEAN | baby |
| WHEEN | a fair number of ("a wheen of dogs") |
| WHIN | gorse, or a kind of stone |
| WHIN SCREE | slope covered with loose stones and rocks |
| WIREWORM | larva of click beetle |
| | |
| YIN | one |